A Sting in the Ale

Colin Devine

Published by Clink Street Publishing 2023

ISBN:
978-1-915229-98-4 - paperback
978-1-915229-99-1 - ebook

TRUST

Like a wandering child beneath a barren landscape,
You trust and step forward with an innocent hope.

Your ancient Chinese eyes speak serious wisdom
Whilst from the shadow of your soul shines no womanly love,

But rather a still and haunting child-like affection
Give future and substance to your fatherless dreams.

Why then must grieve this weary story?
Why then must you lave through the dull and empty doorway?

Affliction

or

Littlestin's Luck

The early evening sun settled itself on the near, low horizon like a recently bloodied nose or the rheumy eye of some ageing wino.

'You've got to'ave yer Tucker,' said fat Steve, emphasising each syllable as they bowled along the walk way between the grey asphalt towers of the accommodation block. The light in the windows flickered weak yellow in the blue haze of the fading evening.

'You've got to 'ave yer Tuc-ker,' said fat Steve once again. His bottom lip curling under his top expressed a mode of pensive aggression.

'I *think* I agree with you.' His companion's name was Littlestin (a curious moniker – but one he was stuck with) and he was much given to 'philosophical' speculations on the least possible pretexts; but on this occasion his tentative fitful tugging at a Black Sobranie gave the lie to his ingrained neurotic, faltering attempts at urban sophistication.

'Nah this spider,' continued Steve as he manoeuvred his portentous hulk towards the concrete step that led to the union bar.

'Nah, this spider sat in the corner of that bathroom, on its nest, on its jack jones for free(three) weeks. Annit never 'sd nuffin to eat, annits still alive? 'Ow do they manage?' Ow do they manage?'

His little companion finally managed a long drawn-out inhalation and exhalation of the poisonous gas from the Black Russian, proving to himself at least, if not to the health-conscious world, that here at least was a man of substance and weight, the curling smoke giving outward sign of cool, complete and inward vision, of a brief hiatus before a conclusion in life is definitely reached.

'Yoga,' he said, stabbing the air casually with his cigarette. 'It must be practising some kind of yoga, an inner conserving of the vital forces. In short, an echo-friendly arachnid.'

'Irac wot?' said Steve absently. Littlestin grimaced at the misheard, mispronounced word as they both wheeled (they were moving at a cracking pace like two comrades on a mission) left then right then left again into the Union Bar.

'Right,' said Steve. 'Let's see if we can find some dosh.'

The Union Bar was a curious structure, an unhappy hybrid of aircraft hangar, airport waiting lounge and disused underground car park; it was an example, a foretaste of socialist realist anti-planning at its most hideous and bleak. Surrounded by such unimaginative and uninspired concrete our hero, this doppelgänger, this almost afterthought from a more generous and optimistic age felt swamped, weary and desolate. He was not a happy man; he was not unhappy. He just was not happy.

'I'm not happy,' he confided.

'You're never 'appy,' said Steve, gazing into the far distance for potential victims. 'Let's see if we can find some dosh. I'll take that side of the bar, you take this one.'

Steve pushed off and left Littlestin standing; lost almost as he fell back on his meagre inner reserves.

The architect should have been castrated at birth, mused our hero. However, this particular architectonic grievance was not the cause of his general state of dissipated disaffection. To be sure, there seemed to be no nameable cause whatsoever, not one you could put your finger on, for his continuing condition of buoyant and self-sustaining misery. A condition that was, moreover, almost the very essence of his being, that wafted from the pores of his skin like a delicate but resilient fragrance, that hung in the very recesses of his psyche like an ingratiating November fog – damp and persistent.

It was not as if he had taken a conscious decision to be miserable. To be sure there were long periods of time when he was completely oblivious of the fact of this morbid disposition. That is to say until someone gave him a poke, a jerk with a stick and woke him up.

There he would sit in a public bar in a public house or in a cafeteria in one of the less celebrated department stores – gently musing on the ironies of life, supremely aware of the surreptitious hand of a grinning fate waylaying both man and muse to a common destiny. He would just be on that point of feeling all warm and rosy inside, amused at the concerns of 'lesser beings without-the-law' when one of their number would interject.

'Cheer up mate, the world doesn't end 'til Thursday' or some such remark. And it would be no good. The game was up and the whole pyramid of cards, the linguistic and metaphorical mirrors of self- delusion would shatter, revealing once more that poverty and despair, the tedious yawning void were of the essence of life and that a comfortable boredom were the sole limits of a sensible life. And back would come the misery and back would come the consciousness of misery in all its naked and unremitting force.

'I'm not happy,' he thought, 'but I don't know why.'

The ambience of the Union Bar did not help matters. Indeed he felt that the bleak and unprepossessing surround was not only matched but surpassed the materialistic nullity and ideological corpse-mongering that passed itself off as mental culture and social concern. Indeed, he was angry and disaffected by the angry and disaffected and with those who sort their future careers in the profession of the same. There was good reason for this – though it could not be precisely defined.

During his first year he had entertained a brief relationship with a young woman of Easter European descent. She had a somewhat dour aspect. A 'somewhat dour aspect' as a descriptive phrase was indeed somewhat too kind. The fact of the matter was, that by all conventional standards known to civilised man she was little short of plug ugly. Nevertheless, our hero, no stickler for convention at the best of times, was unfettered. The fact that she was guilty of a nose that spread itself generously across her the middle distance of her lower face, forming sort of pendulous bridge linking each substantial earlobe; that her eyes (bloated to the shape of fake oriental by some unmentionable childhood disease) were at least five inches apart and that her hair was so thin as to allow at a liberal distance for the counting of each individual strand, was of no matter. Our hero was made of sterner stuff.

His essential characteristics had been formed at a time when it was fashionable for young men to pull and strain at the social leash of background and origin, be this either plebeian or bourgeois. Indeed unconsciously he counted himself among the last of a rich if short-lived tradition of pimply faced post-war renegades in rebellion for something... for something else... for something other... for something god knows what, it all came to the same thing in the end. For Buddha and Krishna, for Karl Marx and Sitting Bull, Trotsky, Modigliani and Gauguin. But it was fading and it was fading fast and he knew it. She on the other hand was 'something else' (as they would say in the fifties). OTHER! She was foreign and posh and for Littlestin that was enough.

A spectator haunts every generation – sorry – I'll type that again. A spectre haunts every generation, a spectre haunts youth – the spectre of middle age. This fiend may of course take various forms; be it either a bit of banter with the Huns, romantically dodging mustard gas in some far-flung field that will remain forever England; or be it the successful detonation of a small nuclear apparatus.

The onward march of time was and is unrelenting and our hero, pushing thirty (though he told himself he looked much younger) was not insensible to its law nor dead to its fatal logic.

She, on the other had, was almost a decade younger. She at least promised some sort of youthful postponement.

And although he was not quite free of his adolescent diffidence with a new prospect (he often wondered who indeed enjoyed such felicity) – apart from Felicity that is – he made his moves quickly quietly and successfully. But he was not a total cynic. The intellectual rapport and emotional warmth that existed between them was real enough. The mutual attraction they established between them spoke of something else than ere sensual desire.

Indeed it seemed to him at time that the apparent vulnerability of her youth and the unaffected candour of her manner – a sure sign of a trusting and untried soul – were of the very essence of the beautiful and the good.

And like a freshly laid carpet of snow that awaits the tramp, tramp and trudge of human all too human feet – she offered herself.

But it was no good, as a long-term arrangement it was no good. Her child-like affection was all too much for him and his aged jaded cynicisms. It was not as if her solicitude were piercing his barrier self-protection; a device formed in the heat of former love relations with other less kind and indeed less innocent of her gender, so much as undermining its general effectiveness. Her unwitting affection had the effect of a corrosive agent and the armour plating slowly and surely began to dissolve.

Our hero. Littlestin to his friends. And I think by now he would count as amongst his friends; our hero did the decent thing. Being of a considerate nature – he waited until the correct psychological moment. In this case the conclusion of exams, then unceremoniously (some would say brutally) pushed her aside.

She returned to Poland and mother, tried unsuccessfully to commit suicide, failed, spent eighteen months nursing her grievance and was ever seen in Littlestin's part of England again.

Littlestin meanwhile, rubbed his hands, breathed out a sigh relief, breathed in a heady draught of intoxicating freedom's fresh air and looked round for fresh pickings in pastures untried.

(He was never far from his agricultural past.)

But alas, trouble was afoot. In the interim, unbeknown to him – all innocence and outmoded expectation her friends, the angry and disaffected, the deprived and starving darlings of the international professional classes on the one hand the flower of the English lower middle class on the other, rallied round.

According to their spokesperson. An Amazonian six-foot pipe smoking (she was six foot not the pipe you understand) Scandinavian Marxist of inclusive inclinations. According to her, not only was Littlestin an heterosexual male (in some circles that was damnation enough) but typically lumpen pleb/sexist/exploiter of the superior sex into the bargain basement of secular sins.

And he was unaccountably hurt. Indeed on his on turf was seen as somewhat 'radical' if not 'progressive'. As a life-long antiracist, to be labelled with a parallel prejudice hurt him more than he could say. The injustice! The cruelty! He was unprepared for and outmanoeuvred by this exercise in social one-upmanship (Upwomanship?), this broadside in calumny and snobbery that hid itself beneath the convenient carapace of political correctness and equalitarian sentiment.

Perhaps it was just his overwrought imagination, tortured by such grief, but it did seem to Littlestin that since that time his fortunes, academic, emotional, sexual or otherwise had taken a faltering but steady downward turn. He therefore felt cheated and angry at the angry and disaffected. However, he was no friend of the established order either; so for the moment at least he was stuck with it. He heaved a sigh of relief and sat down at the nearest table.

A pretty young girl was speaking.

'Women are oppressed,' she said. 'We're all treated like shit.'

Her beautiful, long straw blonde hair fell gracefully over her right shoulder. Bright, shinning intelligent eyes at times flashed invitingly and her well-fed Hogarthian roseate complexion seemed to give the lie to this cant utterance; this wholly hackneyed phrase that spilled from her rosebud mouth like so much second-hand dust, as a merely rhetorical, learnt resentment, like base intrusion into the surrounding air.

'How could anyone but an idiot,' he thought, 'treat you with anything less than respect?'

He leant across the table, carefully avoiding the soggy, beer-stained pamphlets of the politicos and asked, 'Excuse me but could I put a question to you? How would you define oppression exactly?'

This product of privilege had the air of the well-heeled sub-urbs, of spacious gardens in sweeping avenues, of sunny, happy Sunday afternoons. In an earlier age she would have been the subject of adoring paintings by Monet or Reynolds. Her presence spoke volumes of a house with generous bay windows, of holidays in esoteric climes and of an easy facility with parents, teachers and other figures of established authority.

Her eyes flickered as if suddenly started awake. 'No,' she said decisively, 'how would **you** define oppression?' She smiled broadly pleased at her quick reposte, her white teeth gleaming like a Vogue cosmetic ad.

He should have not been let down by her reply. Wealth has no power to purchase penury.

'I would define oppression thus,' he said in mock professorial mode, putting the tips of his fingers, steeple-like, together and then counting off each point in turn for pseudo-seminarian effect.

'One. Not having enough resources at one's fingertips to realise immediate need. I speak of course from first-hand experience of the same. And two, not having the wherewithal to effect in concrete terms long-term projects or desires etc. etc.'

He sat back and felt almost exhausted by what he felt at bottom to be a futile attempt at communication. There was no immediate reply, indeed three was no reply at all and silence fell for a few moments before Littlestin launched himself forward over the table and stuttered.

'Um ah, speaking of which, you couldn't lend me the price of a pint could you?'

But it was no good. He could see it was no good even before he had come to the end of his pathetic request. Her faced drooped. It visibly drooped. The threat of real if trivial need (not trivial to Littlestin however) exposed a moral hiatus, a redundancy if you will and she was not disposed to thank him for this intrusion into her ethically cosy world of untried sentiment. Humanity is a concrete not an abstract proposition, but here and now, at this dreary table, on this dreary evening it was all too much to ask and it was no good. It would not wash. A smattering of left of field undergraduate posturing was no match for mother and a lifetime's prudent conditioning(look after the pennies da de da).

Her reply, was immediate, non-thinking, instinctive and direct. 'I don't think I have any money myself.'

She delivered her denial with a just perceptible air of superiority (such as would be allowed in a student bar) that nevertheless echoed volumes in the hollow shrine of Littlestin's destitute pride. He felt as hopeless and as bottomless as the empty glass into which he was staring.

She took her bags, her beer and turned away from him to address herself to the pressing needs of the pig farmers in Honduras.

It was not as if he chose to be miserable. He lit his last Sobranie and threw the empty pack onto the beer-reeking table.

''ad any luck?' beamed fat Steve as he squeezed past the tables towards Littlestin.

'Nah,' drawled Littlestin finally abandoning all pretence of 'urbane sophistication'.

'So wot 'appened to this spider then?'

The Sobranie pack drifted, turned this way and that on the thin pool of beer and finally slid of the table.

Sonia

Jovanovich was a poor man but he was not a wicked man. It seemed to him that all his life he had been ignored by the world of men and also shunned by the world of women. But the flame of passion and the light of reason needed the substance of the world on which to feed if they were not to altogether disappear. And indeed, on many occasions, poor as he was, he had stood next to and conversed with the abyss that embodied such extinction.

He had stood next to and known many tramps. He had looked into the eyes of desolation and destitution and felt the chill air of pathetic madness from inside their hollow skulls and he was afraid. He was not frightened of them, but rather frightened of himself, least he should go their way.

He was a young man and evidenced all the charm of youth; but he was a man whose history was against him.

We need not say why his history was against him, for genesis of his misfortune does not bear directly on our story.

Suffice it to say that he had done nothing wrong or criminal in the legal sense of the term. Rather, he had unwittingly, owing to misplaced youthful illusions, omitted to perform such actions as were considered right and in conformity with general expectation. And though anger and disappointment were the sleeping partners of his soul he had nevertheless resolved to avoid the pernicious contagions of these syphilitic emotions. At all costs he had resolved not to forget how to love and forgive; even if in the process he found himself despised.

Although Jovanovich lived in a village near a large town – and in between short spells of casual teaching (he had obtained his degree on the strength of a church scholarship reserved for the poorer classes) between periods of casual teaching he would do little else besides wander the streets of the town, half enjoying and half despairing over the sights he saw there. And like a sort of Rameau's Nephew, he struck up secret solipsist relations with the daughters and wives of the local burghers. Relations that were all the more poignant and certainly delightful in their never having seen the light of a conventional morning; for their never having been sullied by trivia and for their never having been consummated and then betrayed by the materiality of the mundane.

For hours at a time, wholly absorbed by the nape of a neck or the swish and frou-frou of a long elegant dress as it swept along the pavement, he would follow, entranced, one or more of these delightful female creatures.

He of course had his favourite spots; his favourite seat in his favourite cafe window, looking out onto the main thoroughfare and his favourite girl.

It need hardly be said that he, of course, new nothing of him.

She only came and went between her father's house (her mother was either dead or had 'disappeared' sometime before) and her school. She came and went gaily each day. She was sometimes by herself or at other times with her friends, chatting and laughing with girlish enthusiasm.

And each time she came near where Jovanovich sat, his little flame of light and love was caught in the refreshing wind of her passing presence and it grew. And it grew into an almost perceptible light. And he harboured this light like a religious offering, like a votive, it was as if the shabby burden of his life had been temporarily lifted from him, as if he had been 'saved' and called from another shore. If she could exist in this world then goodness and beauty existed in this world and truth would not be betrayed. Or so it seemed to Jovanovich.

Her name was Sonia. Sonia Antovich and her father's name was Michailaromanov Antovich. Michael Michailaromanov, among his own circle, was a noted figure in the town. He was chief architect and sat on the board of governors of the school and was also President of the Council of Elders. Not that his occupation of this office stood for much. Although the town was large, it was still only a provincial cluster, more like an extended village; most of the inhabitants had either not heard or, if they had heard, could not care about the house of Antovich. The townspeople were workers, peasants, small shop keepers, tradesmen of various descriptions and they kept themselves much to themselves.

However, notwithstanding his fleeting professional associations, Jovanovich, in a half-casual, half-serious manner, made it his business to know about Sonia and her little world. He read the papers when the exam results were published – he followed her progress through school and noted whenever she attended the opera or local theatre.

He even, one dreary, rainy November afternoon, took the trouble to trace her family history in the reading room of the local library. It would seem she had some minor aristocratic connections on her mother's side whilst her father's heritage was lost in the obscurity of bad debts and wilful bohemianism.

Sonia had this air, and air of abandon and communion with the earth and of exuberant acceptance of anything and everything which was indissolubly linked with an almost absolute self-assurance of and sense of right. It was as if when she took from the world (which she frequently did) she was rather conferring on it the gift of her attention and grace of her presence. And this; for Jovanovich, was her fascination, her charm and perhaps even her poison!

The day, the day he would always remember started like any other. Like a guilty, unwanted quest the wan, pathetic light of a November dawn slipped through the latticed blind. The sickly yellow presence slowly filled the room and seemed to shale his frail body by the shoulders – shuddering he awoke.

He always woke early, even during his short career as a secondary school teacher, when the brutalities of the coming days might counsel the contrary, he always woke early. He had once read that in order to gather energy from the terrestrial and cosmic forces, the astral body, during sleep, detaches itself from the physical, but that prior to proper wakefulness the astral body had not fully re-engaged the corporeal. On this morning, from personal experience, Jovanovich felt he could confirm such speculations. He lay there in a sort of blank awareness, as if his body was a leaden weight and it was with great effort that he dragged himself from the shadows of slumber that morning.

He prepared breakfast, ate it, put on his overcoat, went across the room, down the stairs, across the scullery, his boots echoing on the shiny flagstones, pushed open the heavy wooden doors and stepped out into the fresh, clear morning.

As he walked along the keen wind seemed to carve his face against the alabaster blue sky like a relief by Pico Mirandola. He made his way instinctively, unconsciously towards the town centre. He did not hurry, he always took his time. But through field, hedgerow and copse, his wanderings were without intention.

Apart from his secret solipsist meeting with Sonia he had no idea where he was going; so it was well into the clear autumn morning towards midday before he reached his 'destination'.

He preferred this on many days – simply to wander his free mind unfocused and unfazed by the nagging imperialism of the necessary.

And this indeed was the unacknowledged privilege of the poor, the wealth of the underprivileged and the divine responsibility of the apparently irresponsible. He was, in his own mind the Saint of the Spontaneous gesture and it was his self-appointed role to remind all men of the fundamental freedom they embodied or could be if they took the chance.

And for this he was despised and shunned by the world of men but also by the word of women. For they did not want to be reminded of what they were or of what their possibilities might be and the profound responsibilities thereof but rather preferred the artificial slavery, pain and self-importance of being what they were not. Self- betrayal, the social falsehood at every level, is always an easy option, and even philosophers had their schools and pupils to hide behind. But he had no schools, no pupils, no doctrine, nothing to teach and even less desire to do so. Indeed, our hero despised the professions, regarded teaching as nothing more than a sophisticated form of brainwashing and loathed the idea of any sort of trade. And so he stood for man alone. For naked non-accommodated man and was shunned and feared. The watery cowardice in the glancing eye. This was how he thought and rationalised to himself to himself; for well he knew he knew, in his clearer moments of self-doubt and despair, that his little self-aggrandizing theories of nature, man and freedom were but feeble attempts to reconcile the irreconcilable and to accept the unacceptable.

Across a few glistening morning meadows, round the edge of the copse tramped Jovanovich until he presently came to the edge of the town – to the poorer quarters. He wandered down the dismal back streets and turned into a long alley that led to the bustling thoroughfares and the promise of Sonia. In reality the alley was a walkway between semi-derelict outhouses and a few disused workshops. It smelt of damp cardboard, rotten wood and decaying redbrick work that epitomised the squalid underbelly of urban existence.

However, when this way led to a possible meeting with Sonia – the decaying brickwork and rotting woo partook of the Autumnal hues of rich if unknown foliage; the wet flagstones shone with a preternatural light and he felt moved to a condition of quiet joy and inner expectation.

'Oiii. Ack ack ack. Ahh.'

Jovanovich stopped. He was startled and almost frightened. In a dim doorway sat an old man crouched over, hugging his knees for warmth. His filthy raincoat was trailing in the puddles and mud. His beard was awash with saliva and bits of old food and Jovanovich could see amongst the bristles thousands of lice glistening like quicksilver fish in the cold morning air. Jovanovich had seen derelicts like this before but he had never seen derelicts like *this* before.

'Young man,' the old man's voice was course and bronchial. 'Young fella – you're educated young sir…'

'Yes' said Jovanovich – not thinking. 'Well no not really, what's the matter?'

The old man held a piece of string in his hand – a long piece of string the led through a doorway into disued shop. 'Take this.' The old man clutching the piece of string, waved his trembling fist in the air. 'Take this – look after her.'

Jovanovich gently removed the string from the old man's grasp – and as he did so he felt the fist stiffen and fall with an indifferent clunk onto the paving stone. Jovanovich jumped back slightly. To his immediate horror he realised he had just witnessed his first death(he hoped it would be his last). The pathetic tramp had indeed died. Jovanovich was stunned but he did not panic and the cold fear that passed over him was soon gone. He was not afraid of death of or any of life's absolutes. It was life as it was lived in its relative aspects that frightened him and he was frightened of Sonia. The whoring, warring world of the criminal did not frighten, he was familiar with that, he was almost at home with that but he was still frightened of Sonia.

As he slowly pulled the long piece of string towards him, he heard a BAAAAR and the clanking of plaintive bell from inside the hollow darkness of the destitute shop. It must have been the recent shock but he seemed to be pulling for an immeasurably long time when a tiny ghost of whiteness appeared in the empty doorway. It sheened and shimmered as slowly, slowly the shy animal stumbled forward until its pointed little face and twitching ears were full visible against the surrounding darkness. Jovanovich crouched down and the animal placed its cold nose onto his. Strange it was how he felt himself melting inside and strange the peculiar swollen vision of the animal's body. It was a goat very far gone in pregnancy.

The sad bleating of its hollow chords and the clang-clang at that moment seemed to come at Jovanovich like the haunting melody of half-forgotten tune. He stooped down at whispered, 'Well, little mate, your owner is dead I'm afraid and you can bleat all you like. Tell you truth I feel like bleating myself sometimes. Feel a bit lost m'self. I won't tell the cops about the old man.

They'll find him soon enough. Besides he's dead and I can't help him now and those nitwits at the station will take up too much of my time.'

And so it was that Jovanovich emerged into the bright street, into the bright sunshine of the cold Autumn morning.

He tethered his new companion outside the cafe and took his normal place near the window and waited for Sonia. And when she came she came bringing flowers. Despite his outward composure the events of the morning had left him feeling drained and rather weary. With a sense of dissolute abandon and dismissal he surveyed the people coming and going down the thoroughfare.

The businessmen, the rather bored-looking street vendor and the scurrying insurance clerks and petty government officials(the latter a pathetic parody of respectability and business efficiency). And amidst all this provincial bustle an old man's life had slipped away – unknown, unwanted and unmourned.

A light had gone out in the eternal night and the darkness paid no regard – but rather checked the time, took memos from one room and one office to another, made plans, put on a dress and took off a dress and preened itself in every half reflection in very window. And, and… and then she came, flouncing over the hill at the end of the street, turning into the walk way, laughing gaily with her friends – her glowing face all sunshine and smiles. And like fresh flowers and sparkling meadows she descended into the gloom that was Jovanovich. He just met her glance as he looked up over his coffee cup – and she just turned away in time – but they both knew they had met. Her little gay band had stopped by the vendor just opposite the coffee shop and being on the outside this eager cluster of young womanhood she was distracted for a second and looked round. And then she saw it – she saw the goat standing outside the shop, a forlorn little creature lost in the busy street – and Sonia's face at once bloomed into an ocean of warmth and feminine solicitude. She approached the beast slowly, as if afraid, and with an almost tender stealth crouched down beside it – stroking its wet muzzle and limp ears.

'Hello, little sweetie, little beauty' she hummed. 'What brings you to town today?

'Do you like her?' It was Jovanovich speaking. The bizarre events of the morning had had a strange effect on him and no one was more surprised than himself that he should behave left his set without thinking and was asking her this question. After all he was only Jovanovich the 'junkie' (as he was unkindly known and slandered). He felt himself blushing slightly so he shoved his hands into his long overcoat pockets and buried his head beneath his high collar.

'Yes' she said, looking brightly into his face.

'Yes,' he said, crouching down. 'She's lovely, isn't she?' He pulled the long ears playfully as the goat butted his side.

Sonia all at once became aware of the heavy presence of Jovanovich; of his thick tweed overcoat, old, second-hand, slightly dirty and smelling of tobacco, of the creased and crumpled walking boots and of his plenteous greasy hair. She was not sure of her emotions but she pulled away from his nearness and stood up.

'Does she belong to you?' she said, looking down on both of them. Her voice was not cold but it lacked a certain enthusiasm.

'I suppose so,' he said rather timidly; he was struggling with his natural diffidence. 'Yes, yes, it does – somebody gave her to me, I'm supposed to look after her.'

'Well, I hope you do,' she said slightly emphasising each word as if it were an order. 'I'm sure you will.'

There was a moment of clumsiness and she lightly turned and began to walk back to her fiends saying simply, 'Goodbye.'

'Umm old on a sec,' stuttered Jovanovich without knowing what he was going to say next. 'Umm.' He shifted from foot to foot like a guilty school boy. 'Um, look if you'd like to come and see her you can come at any time. I live in the village – you can come and feed her if you want. Everybody knows me there, in the village that is.'

He felt a fool but could not stop now that he had started. 'Just ask for Jovanovich the Junkie.'

'Yes, ok maybe I will.' She smiled. 'Yes. Sure. thanks.'

She turned once again and ran off to join her friends who had moved further down the street. Jovanovich felt as if he were blooming inside, as if a bright flower were opening inside him, opening up in the darkness of his fluttering soul.

The garden at the back of house of Jovanovich was untended. Indeed, it was more scrubland than garden. A patch of wasteland covered with tufts and clusters of thick winter grass, bordered at the bottom by a wide but shallow stream. This stream wound round the backs of the old wooden houses, skirted the copse and meandered through the centre of the village. To get to his house one could either take the conventional route through the town and over the packhorse bridge at the edge of the village or one could come straight across the meadows and wade through the stream.

Jovanovich often took this latter route in the summer but could not remember on this day which route he had taken home, the bridge or the stream; hi mind was so full of a fragrant female image.

The term 'Bramdays' the age-old custom of gathering in the victuals against the coming winter. Traditional there were thirteen 'Bramdays' before the festival of the week of the winter lights. As that day was the first of the thirteen the goat was duly named Bramvich to celebrate the event of their meeting and to remind Jovanovich of the first words between Sonia and himself.

Jovanovich gave Bramvich the remains of the previous day's stew and tethered her to the stake on the scrub land at the back of the house. The autumn evening drew on apace and Jovanovich took his usual meagre repast – lit one or two candles and then settled down to his latest study – a short history of Russian literature.

The wind slapped playfully around the gable end of his attic room and he could hear the pleasant clang clang of Bramvich's bell as she gadded about in the hollow dark.

At first it was a tiny spark – a bleating beating heart against the hostile stars, a sensation that was almost at first imperceptible, as if the inside of his skull were being slowly layered in cotton wool. As if an animal had made its bed at the base of the bowl bed inside his cranium; he could smell its arm flesh and feel its pulsating veins pressing at the back of his eyes. And somebody was tolling the bell of Saint Peter in his head and he could see nothing for a few seconds but an ocean of white hair that was dissolving slowly, slowly in the inky air.

Like one of those self-illuminating fish that live on the ocean floor, Sonia came swimming up to him out of the blackness. Laughing cruelly, she kept clapping her hands and pushing and pushing and shoving and blowing and laughing, taking wicked delight at the stammering attempts of this newcomer to her world. Sonia's father, Michel Michailaromanov came floating up, his thick black moustache glistening in the wetness of the black void. His voice, an intonation of the St. Peter's bell; along, long drone, heavy with the world and its chronic despair.

Sonia continued to cavort and clap, pushing down, pushing, pushing down; there's another peasant for the pot, another oik for the ointment, another peasant gone and pushing and blowing, blowing as if she were trying to put out a whole birthday cake of candles. And then there was nothing but the smell of smoking tallow as slowly, slowly the smoke drifted upwards and resolved itself into a place of illumination. Just an empty space… A piece of scrub land with tufts of winter grass billowing grass, boarded at the bottom by a shallow stream. On the far side stood Sonia, weeping for a votive light and a throat cut and a belly ripped. Out flopped a dead red foetus, as dead as it's mother but with a gash where a heart should be. And where a heart should beat and flesh should meet a father's hand squeezed and released, squeezed and released and the kid jerked its eyes awake, open.

'Sonia, Sonia, come quick, it lives.'

Splashing and running through the silver water she came whilst the heavens opened up and like thick twisting ribbons of satin, down the rain poured hiding her tears and plastering her hair to her face.

'Yes, yes it lives.' In a small Russian town.

But her smile through the rain was like sunlight.

Rap. Rap. Rap.

Someone was throwing stones. Rap. Rap. He stumbled awake from the chair, his book fell to the floor as he reached for the window, struggled with the latch, opened it and shoved his head out into the clean morning air. The breeze, cold and stinging, caught him fresh in the face and the shadows of the night fell immediately from him.

'Hey, hello, it's me, you said I could come, remember?'

Sonia stood astride the tufts of winter grass in the garden below, shielding her eyes from the weak sun with her cupped hands – looking up.

There was a chivvying, almost arrogant note in her voice.

'Remember?'

'Yes,' said Jovanovich, yes, yes, of course.

Where she stood the gentle rain spangled the grass with silver whispers of light.

City Lights

There's a woman on the stairs
Who says she really cares
A kid in a dirty rain coat.
There's a man in the can
who knows all her affairs
And smiles as you hand him the bank notes.
City lights city girls on the corner
Hit the night, hit the world hit the heat
City Lights but it's too late to warn her
Not so sweet where those pretty girls meet…

Like the Sun

It was Sunday afternoon, late afternoon, hot, sticky and close. For some reason the stranger could not divine all the bars, those cute little affairs on the corner of each street not normally so full to light and life were closed and dead to his desires. He walked quickly and sometimes almost ran from one end of the block to another but his search seemed vain and fruitless. Instead of light and life the death silence of steel grey shutters bared his petty pleasures, denied his desires and he felt the meanness inside him to begin to rise. Sweating slightly – he was in a hurry – a few streets away blue-black clouds were bunching up over the tops of the uptown high-rise office blocks. In the afternoon sun their concrete and glass facades were glowing yellow against the violent blue-black backdrop of the threatening storm. The air, in stagnant anticipation, was waiting for something to break. A distant grumble and the first fat arrow heads of rain began to smack, smack and sizzle on the parched pavement.

The stranger, desperate to escape the coming downpour ducked in and out the cars down several side street until he saw in the far distance a sign saying **BAR** winking through the steaming rain like an old hooker standing in a doorway. Still dodging through the lazy traffic, he skipped across the street, pushed through the closed double doors. He gave a start when they when they unexpectedly clanged/banged shut behind him.

Forty pairs of dark brown eyes turned to greet him, turned to inspect him with the silent interrogative gaze of the habitually suspicious. The hostile regard for the unexpected, uninvited guest.

You **HERE?** 'What?' 'Why?'

The sallow faces of the high cheeked-boned creoles seemed surprised at his presence to the point of taking offence; a sourness seemed to mix with the smell of coffee, sweat and cigarettes.

The buzzing of flies round broken lampshades in the sudden hush. There was negativity in the air.

From a cavern deep within him, the only white man in the 'gin joint' felt the first stirrings, the first fear and trembling of rising panic. Mad blind bats began to unfurl themselves from his innards and swirl themselves against the side of his ribcage and the palpitating walls of his now thumping heart. Flight or fight? Without thinking the stranger strode towards the bar, hoisted himself onto bar stool and ordered a drink.

'Una cana por favour, y un bocadillo tambien.'

'Si, senore.'

The mad bats turned into precious peacocks strutting on summer lawns.

Settling down and glancing to his left the stranger caught the intense of his creole neighbour. Warm brown velvet set in a lake of liquid marble-beautiful – but full of hate.

Inca hate. Pueblo hate. Hate of the eternally displaced and dispossessed. Holy grail of your mother's shit hate.

Outside the window the torrent of rain was smashing the pavement like an avalanche of breaking glass. Each man appraised the other steadily for some seconds. They held a cold glance for a moment and then the stranger turned his attention to his beer.

'The shit shell of your mother,' he thought. 'Tough luck if you've had a bad day or even bad life. You've got the wrong bloke mate. White guilt means nothing to me. You think life's easy because you have blue eyes. And my eyes are not blue.'

Further down the bar two middle-aged men – skilled artisans of some description – were fooling around – playfully slapping each other's faces and giving mock punches to their respective bellies. They were joshing one another in a strong patois the stranger did not really understand and did not care to follow.

He sipped his beer and thought, not for the first time that day, of the beautiful señorita he had met the morning. He sat and thought of her.

'ZZZZZ' the intercom buzzed his admittance like an angry wasp as he pushed hard on the wrought ironwork of the heavy door, baroque tracery protecting cheap yellow frosted glass as he almost fell into the vacant pool of the dark entrance. A little way ahead the musty smell of the stairwell was dank and uninviting. From somewhere in the bowels of the building the sound of 'La vie en Rose' curled plaintively through the air. From the cheap radio the sharp bitter voice of the 'little sparrow' scrapped the dusty air like a badly played violin. The revolving tune kept flashing in and out of focus like the glint of a lighthouse in a smothering fog. The stranger felt oppressed, apprehensive. The architecture of the stairwell (industrial brutalism at its worst) did not help his sense of unease. In the semi-darkness the stairs, landing and crude concrete columns, like an arachnid's den spun by a spider on acid, seemed a lattice-work of missed opportunities. Not sure of his bearings he walked down the hallway and gingerly began to climb the first flight of stairs.

As he turned the corner of the first landing he heard the dull click of a switch somewhere above him. From the next floor soft ray of light, warm orange in the darkness, fell across his face and into the vacant spaces below. Looking upwards, he climbed towards the figure standing in the doorway. Framed in the warm orange light she seemed to him like silent Russian icon or Balinese shadow puppet poised at the second of being twitched into action. She wore a simple dress of black lace. She was elegant. The icon spoke. The puppet moved.

'Hola carino, pase aqui, pase aui.' By way of invitation she stepped back into the arrow hallway and with gentle downward movement of her right hand waved him into the small but neat apartment. There was a tapestry hanging on the wall and red orchids in a white vase on a small table. A smell of apples, lemons and freshly baked bread twisted through the air.

'Estoy esperando para ti.' She had a strong accent with which he was not familiar. Not Spanish and yet…

He squeezed past her in the hallway and turned into the little room. She followed him and as she did so the light caught her face and for the first time he became aware of her delicacy. Her tanned skin was smooth like translucent china and her dark eyes were almost oriental in their narrowness. A slight smile seemed to play round her lips and eyes, pearls of dark velvet set in translucent marble, sparkled iridescent in the dim light. They seemed to laugh. The thick sheen of her 1920s bob cut, black like a Raven's wing, shimmered purple and green rainbows as she walked around the room. She sat down opposite him with the hands of her outstretched arms resting purposefully on her knees.

Her gaze seemed to fall on him like an instruction.

'Ahora, estmos aqui, I believe you have something for me?'

'Si,' said the stranger as he realised he could say no more. Transfixed as he was. He shoved his hand into his pockets and drew out a small round silver tin – embossed with a snake' head.

'Aqui here you are,' he said in school boy Spanish. He felt a catch in his voice.

A mistake. It was all a mistake. In his inner eye this young woman was as missed placed as a thin gazelle mincing round a bullring or a peacock stepping artfully through the mud of a pigsty. He had a strong feeling that she did not belong here and that he, also, was out of place. Their conversation began to fumble.

'Seora Ramirez sent you?'

'Yes,' he said stupidly, and like a bad actor he felt his mouth begin to dry.

However, her sparkling eyes met his, with her scarlet-painted thumbnail she prized open the snake's head lid from the silver tin. She dabbed the white powder with the tip of her cocked little finger, her eyes gazing intently into his, dusted the white powder on the end of her glistening tongue.

'MMMMM' bueno, bueo, blnco ora, white gold.' She laughed and offered him the tin.

'You want some?'

'No I am sorry señora but I have to go.' he began to get up from the bed. She stood up and then rested her hands on his shoulders. 'Porque?'- her dark eyes became darker.

'Porque porque no, no, no entiendo nada,' fumbled the stranger in his 'holiday' Spanish as he tried to pull away from her grip. He stumbled towards the door.

'No es necessario,' she began but he did not let her finish her sentence as he slid through the door. It was a clumsy exit and he looked and felt a fool. Her pained angry voice followed him down the stairwell. She was shouting something in Portuguese in an accent he could now place but not understand, her unintelligibility adding to his confusion; the thought passed over his mind that her patois was the voice of slavery.

He pushed through the door into the gathering storm and stood lost in the fading afternoon light.

Refugees. The world is full of refugees. Tourism. Ersatz refugee status cut price for the affluent. At this moment, sitting at the bar. Stock still like Buddha with beer, the stranger, as sure as any rain sodden poor sod from Sangatte camp northern France was fleeing - fleeing – fleeing. The obscure object of desire was not his problem, she was not obscure but his desires were. He could not escape their debilitating grasp. Only to the superficial did beauty seem superficial. He could not shake her image from his mind. Beauty is not skin deep. It is a presence felt, hidden or disclosed by a chance arrangement of hair, eyes, bone structure, skin and muscles. These are messages from the big fellah, as the Muslims would have us believe, but they are never superficial. Thus far did the stranger console himself. He was not after all an 'ordinary man'. And like a half-remembered tune that reuses to die from the mind, she was still with him. He felt animated by her soul, her shameless presence. This was an absurdity, he knew, because he did not know and would never know her soul. But to think of her that minute – at that dim dirty bar with the buzzing flies and the resentful clientele, the broken lives and broken light shades – was to experience an inner light.

And yet he had walked away. He had turned his back and walked away.

Cradling his beer the stranger silently shadow boxed with his hungry ghosts and wrestled with his angels.

He felt the debilitation of indecision. The power of advertising. To regain the illusion of self-control, man hood and gravitas he took a cigarette from his top pocket. He hated smoking but found the ritual of lighting up a convenient prop. Often the ritual was enhanced if he needed to ask a stranger for a light. Imposing himself on a complete stranger was an affirmation, a minor victory in the impersonal imperialism of everyday life.

He leaned over with a direct look and asked if the resentful Creole had a light; 'Tiene fosforo?' The 'fosforo' was given with a bad grace, and it was a victory for the stranger. He was after all – a little man. The restorative ritual complete, the stranger returned to dancing with his hungry ghosts/demons; returned to wrestling with his angels. He was oppressed by the nagging weight of the possible, could he, should he – see her again? Once the rain outside the window had washed itself away had he the 'courage' to retrace his steps?… do not ask what is I… He knew that if he returned he would regret it. And yet if he did not return… he would regret that also. For an hour or more the vacuous ritual, shifting backwards and forwards on his stool as if impatient for something to happen. of drink, drink, cigarette and drink continued to spiral down the afternoon. The resentful creole at his side became evermore restive. The stranger found him easy to ignore as he sat like an accused suspect in the courtroom of his heart waiting for the invisible verdict. 'Oh, what is it. Let us go and make our visit.'

Using the wall phone beside the bar he made his call.

'Hola, soy yo. Si si es el hombre blanco. Escucha bonita es possibl manana por la manana. Me gusta usted mucho.'

'Si,' came the soft but decisive reply. 'Pero, manan estare diferente. De acuerdo?'

He put the phone down and returned to the bar. The creole had gone – what he had wanted to happen was never going to happen. The fat barman came over, genial for some reason.

Wiping the bar he said, 'Me permite una copa?'

'Si senoe, grazie,' said the stranger, only half aware that he was being offered a drink.

His mind was far distant – recalling the cold catch of a woman's voice.

The storm had flushed itself away half an hour before and the heavy silent heat was beginning to suck the pavements dry. As he ran down the metro steps, he felt the cool air of the conditioning system slap him gently in the face like the welcome caress of a wet flannel. There were a few people standing around on the underground platforms. They looked vacant and lost like those stray mannequins in a painting by de Chirico. He sat down on the marble seat that ran along the metro wall. He felt the cold against his back and legs. After the cool of the street he was grateful for its cool embrace. He laid back and breathed a silent sigh of relief, his mind empty of all hope or expectation.

A decision is a decision after all. It has a certain tranquillising effect – even if one suspects in the dark recesses that the decision is wrong.

He heard the first soft click of a woman's step on the adjacent stair on the opposite platform; they gradually became louder. The click klak, klak, click as she slowly but purposefully walked down the stairs onto the platform. Despite his beer sodden tiredness he looked up and watched her walked to the central bench. She was not young but she was not old. She wore a blue serge suit with a medium skirt and white stockings and dark emerald green shoes. To the stranger's eye she had a modest elegance and he could not but help follow her with his gaze as she took her seat on the bench.

She crossed her legs and the fog of the stranger's mental exhaustion began to lift and unconsciously he began taking notes. Her sallow skin, which had a luxurious light tan and a soft sheen that seemed almost to glow, was stretched taught across high elegant cheekbones. She was not so much weathered by age as worn down by luxury. Pleasure rather than adversity was her hidden enemy. We were all worn away by something. Perhaps pleasure was her wasting disease? The stranger refused to look away as these half thoughts skidded across his vacant mind like insects across the clear surface of a pond. Suddenly she looked up from her magazine and caught his eye; she was obviously aware of his interest. Feeling awkward he sat on his hands and glanced down at his shoe and then pretended to look for something in his inside pocket. Now that he knew she knew he knew he glanced at her again. She was looking down the platform as if expecting someone; but no one came. The with her left hand she began to bunch up her hair and let it fall softly on her shoulders. Brushing some imaginary dust from her skirt she let the other hand rest on her knee. She looked in his direction, scratched the corner of her lip with her painted fingernail, uncrossed her legs, took off her small blue jacket, crossed her legs once more, folded the jacket and laid it carefully across her resting thighs. Again she brushed something from her knee. Smiling gently to herself, she looked down at her feet then swivelled her gaze along the platform once more. The train was coming in… from the opposite platform they both got into the same carriage. He stood in the doorway – steadying himself by the ceiling rail and spying her from the corner of his eye. There was no recognition but just a vague feeling. Once or twice she coughed slightly.

They both got off at Cataluña and she walked just ahead of him. She was walking slowly. When they came to the scrum at the foot of the escalator – she was last in line before he arrived. Across the surface of his aching mind yet another insect thought skidded; was she holding back deliberately? Was he chasing her or was she waiting for **the** moment. Waiting to be caught or awaiting to catch?

Her blouse was cut beneath the shoulder and standing directly behind her on the escalator he could smell her faint scent. Her skin seemed to shimmer with an inner warmth. This was not a woman who had trouble with her sensual nature. She was happy in her skin. She did not need, either from ideology or from fear and misconceived piety to sublimate her world.

As she pushed through the ticket barrier on the Cataluña concourse the stranger was still close behind. She did not hurry.

'Senora?'

'Si.'

She turned and smiled gently at him.

'Donde va usted?'

'Me voy a mi amiga.'

'Quire usted tomar una copa conmigo?'

'No. Lo siento. No pudo Tengo que encontra mi amiga. Pero muches gracias Senore.'

The lady gave such emphasis to the two words muchas graciasthat each one sounded like a kiss. 'Muchas gracias senore, Muchas muchas gracias si pero no.'

But her eyes shone, shone like the sun.

The Hidden Clerks

Do you know what it's like to be a slave?

To be forever tending the beautiful flowers for the iron cross

master-ugly and grey.

Forgotten in your corner of the cinder yard/

Do you know what it's like?

To be never quite up to the mark?

To be never quite it,

To be never quite the thing

To be never one of… Do you?

The intense blue sky of a shimmering June morning

Quietly burnishing the day like a forties old photograph burnt at

the edges – cradled in the black and stink of the fire.

The hedgerows gleaming like thick green bottle glass.

The azul sky, furious like a blue furnace, humming like a hammer

against the hungry skull.

On these days and under these conditions even the brightest flower

has its halo of darkness.

Do you?

You – safe in your job wallah-box life,

Right paces, right places to all the right faces.

Even you, Queen of the photocopier, in your little space,

Jewel of the hidden judgement, celebrated and calibrated for a job

well done, in your tidy world, your clean legal corner.

Even you.

As they say, what goes around comes around.

Even you, bewildered like a lost lamb stumbling through
the night,

one day, screaming from sleep,

Will wake with your halo of darkness.

Tristram Brella's Day

In those days, in that part of the world the sky was like a vast and vacant mirror a wide expanding dome of infinite blue liberation or stagnant weight of infinite grey depression -depending on one's disposition, the time and the seasonal mood of the moment. The earth, the flat monotonous-bleak as the Ukrainian steppe – was merely viewing platform, of the night stars or the scudding clouds by day, swept by the cold winds from across the channel, from the great plains of the Siberian north. The light was cold but clear blue and on a good day in summer everything, the land, the trees, the houses – the milling greedy Saturday crowds in the small towns seemed to be swimming in and made out of an ocean of transparent porcelain. The tangible fragility of the passing moment was all they possessed and all they needed to possess.

In the autumn the air was tinged with a soft russet red; whilst in the evenings a subtle gentle brown fog seemed to cress the damp air.

It was an early afternoon in the late autumn and the worrying wind was turning/churning the dead leaves upwards and upwards in elegant arabesques which then collapsed on themselves and fell to like crazed desperate ballerinas of lost souls looking for a home on the cold earth, in that desolate place, far, far from the milling crowd.

Tristram Brella (Brella to his friends) turned the corner in that small forgotten town (a sniggering bye word in the Metropolis from which he was in temporary absence) at a brisk. Confident and forthright pace – like a soldier on leave and proud of his regiment; chest out, arms swinging, resplendent in his uniform. (Although he was not a soldier – he had been excused cadet training at his minor public school on account of mild asthma – and he was not wearing uniform, nor were his arms swinging.) As he walked, or rather marched along he inhaled deeply the cold autumn air. He loved the madding wind, he loved the slight smell of north – sea ice and salt it carried on its wings, he loved the stark swaying trees, their black branches scratching the sky like gnarled arthritic fingers. The dun-coloured earth? – he loved that too. He was a young man clearly in love with the deep joy of simply being alive (which is to say that nothing in his short life had yet unhinged of his untried satisfactions and assumptions). He was still in love with the magic and myth of the simple gift of being.

In short Tristram Bella, so far, had had a good year. His first term at university had gone well; he had made a few good friends – the childhood traumas of boarding school were forever behind him and he felt pleased with himself, his situation, his circumstance and his progress. He turned another at the same brisk pace. Behind him the dead leaves continued their merry dance. Perhaps they too were in love with life?

'Mr Lee,' the official's voice, worn thin by years of tangling with other people's problems, the sorry mess of their inadequate and unholy lives, could barely conceal its mixture of anger and contempt at the shuddering, hunched up creature he saw sitting before her. Lee's closely cropped hair (number one) looked, in that bright, colour-coordinated office, bristling with CCTV cameras pointed like cannons in all directions, like the mark of Cain, an eternal imposition on the defeated eternal prisoner, rather than its intended act of aggression, its supposed act of defiance, its two-fingered salute to the fuck you world. He was a natural anarchist, although he did not know what the word anarchist meant, all authority was to him anathema. (He did not know the meaning of that word either.)

'Mr Lee,' the official said again; the voice had the arch insistence of an impatient schoolmistress trying to engage the interest of a wayward and inattentive child. No matter to her the chronological maturity of her clients. And sooner or later, after perfunctory politeness – it came around to this – contempt; the cold contempt of the powerful for the weak, the contempt of the rich for the poor, the implied contempt of the happy for the distraught and loveless. Contempt; safe official bullying contempt. It was after all one of the perks of the job. It was after all something to boast about with the girls in the pub after work. The cosy office matiness reinforced the radical otherness of this human detritus of which Mr Lee was a specimen – those inadequate items who were not quite up to the hard business of life.

And there they all were, day after day, begging for her assistance; failures in the fundamental test of life who were doomed that universal condition of childhood – dependence. Demanding monsters of petty egotism, their grubby problems forever sucking at the harsh maternal breast, the cold metal mother of the State.

And at this moment she was the State. And they were her bread and butter – her mortgage, her marriage and her holidays in Spain; and she resented them. She resented them because deep down, somewhere in her shapely body the visceral knowledge of her own dependence chewed and chewed at her soul like a rat chewing the bars of its cage.

'MR Lee' her voice a cold switchblade slicing through silk. 'MR LEE.'

Lee jerked his head up; stared her in the eye. His eye watery, rheumy, indistinct – like his voice. Her eye, cold sharp, almost twinkling with pleasure – the pleasure of power – but not quite – like her tired yet insistent voice. Not quite the thing.

'Want,' he said or rather grunted. It came across as …UNT.

The official sat up sharply, her head tilted to one side.

'I'm sorry,' almost offended now, indignant but not surprised -after all what can one expect…?

'WANT.' This time more forcefully clearly.

'My name is Want' he mumbled through gritted teeth. 'Lee Want not Mr LEE. I'm not fucking Chinese.'

'There is no need to swear, we don't have to tolerate it you know and I can see you're not Chinese.'

'Good.' Exasperated, he had been in the job centre for two and a half hours and was anxious to cut to the chase, come to the point and be of home. He was anxious for them to stop dishing the dirt and start dishing the dosh.

'What I need,' he said slowly in the mistaken belief that she would sympathize and understand, 'What I need is a personal issue.'

'That's just it, Mr. Lee.'

'WANT!' Lee raised his voice almost to a shout. 'My name is fuckun Want.' He was feeling his anger rise from the pit of his stomach, like a skinhead kundalini snake on speed. His hands began to shake.

'Yes. Want, Mr Want,' the official briskly carried on- aware of possible verbal escalation – or something worse (but unlike Mr Lee she was not shaking – she was even stirred – this too was part of the mystery of her calling) whilst the fat security guards (one of them munching a McDonald's, ketchup dripping down his chin) hovered with malice aforethought intent in the background- they too were aware of the perks of the job and that anecdotes and alcohol were backslapping made or each other.

'Mr Want, we cannot issue personal issues at this juncture as we still need proof of identity.'

'But I came here last month – you know who I am.'

'Nevertheless we still need **doc-u-men-tation** her voice hung on every syllable as if it were wet kiss. Lee was aware of her pink lip gloss glistening under the office neon.

Why did she delight in high flown officialese when dealing with the habitually monosyllabic? In the outhouse of her unconscious this half thought flitted like a guilty rat across a dusty floor, gimble eye glinting in the darkness. A slight shudder of pleasure rippled up her spine.

'Do you have passport?' she smiled.

She loved this, the cat and mousetrap duplicity of official concern.

She was fishing and she could feel him bite on her sharp little hook. She already knew hep obsessed no passport but could not resist the fun of reeling him in.

'Naw, I've orlready told yew it ws stolen.'

'A utility bill?' her eyebrows raised in bright concern.

'Naw.' His right hand swung up and down emphasising every word. 'Naw I've orlredy said. I'm sleeping on mate's floor. 'Ow can I get a utility bill?'

'Birth certificate; you must have a birth certificate?'

'Yeah of course but I don't know where it is dew oi? When me mum split from me dad all that sort stuff went out the winda ditit?'

'Well. Go to the town hall and order replacement ad come back here after and we'll see what we can do.'

'But oi need an issue now.'

Hi voice was insistent with the pressure of rising anxiety. He was aware the security guards squaring up and paying attention. Like the average moon-faced squaddies they were anxious to put their training to the test. Lee, who, despite his monosyllabic persona was not entirely stupid, in fact he was not stupid at all, he was anxious to thwart their professional intentions. Also, he could sense the official, Sarah on her lopsided name tag, was not going to be moved by any appeal to the power of reason or his pressing needs. In the universal contest between the power of reason and the reasons of power – the reasons of power always wins; although Lee would not have said as much – and in his desiccated soul he felt like a mountain cigarette eds in swamp of cold tea. Useless and powerless he gave up the fight. He sank.

'Yeh alrioght,' he sighed.

He pushed back the chair, stood up, his limbs and indeed his spirit felt heavy with the patty defeat he had just suffered at the hands of the faded prettiness of this petty official. He caught a faint whiff off her cheap perfume. It seemed to confirm the official claptrap. She turned to the computer screen and began to press a few eyes. It was as if he was no longer in the room. He thought he could detect a faint glimmer of a smile just play across her face as she made the necessary adjustments before taking her break. Another good outcome for the department. Another few brownie points for her nose and another Christmas card from the minister. There would be chuckles by the photocopies this afternoon. The poor old British taxpayer saved once again; the fact that Lee was British and poor had nothing to do with it. This sorry fact seemed to escape everyone's attention.

Down on the farm Lee's grandfather always said.

'No matta wat appen boi yer gotta kip puttun one fut in front of t'other.'

This Lee duly did as he tramped out into the cold autumn air even though his feet felt like lead and were getting heavier by the minute.

'WENDY,' he said to himself as the saw the twenty-five-year-old girl leaning against wall – his spirits lifting slightly.

'WENN,' he called to her across the street.

Wendy, his girlfriend, or Wenn as he called her, had been waiting outside for him for over an hour and was tugging on her last ciggy like staving child sucking at a wasted breast. Her furious knuckles white with cold.

She had the poverty (born of poverty, trash tv and trash tv dinners eaten out of cardboard boxes and testing much the same); she had the poverty of imagination that made her aware of little else save the pressure of her own blinkered need. Her sympathy for her boyfriend (a relationship pinned down by the habits of inertia and fear of loneliness – rather than sustained by affection floating on the warm currents of desire) was so qualified as to be almost non-existent.

'Wot abaeut the fags then, we need sum money f'fags?' she drawled

After he related the results of the meeting with 'fucken bitch in he soch.'

'Mum ell lendus sum till tamora.a fiover til tamora.'

Lee needed some positive female feedback after his bruising encounter with the D.S.S. Dominatrix inside and he went to hold Wenn's hand; but she deftly eluded his endeavours. Turning away she rummaged in her shoulder bag, flicked out a cheap compact mirror and frantically applied some maroon lipstick. She would not reward his failure with the comfort of affection but neither would he jeopardise her only relationship by the rashness of outright rejection. She was too well aware of all the qualities she lacked. The nervous application of makeup was a comfort activity as well as a defence. Cold, gimlet eyed, skin like dry parchment, of a pinched and sour disposition, deep down in her bones, she-instinct and all female, she was still female. She was Nancy who had fallen on even harder times but her man was no Bill Sykes. Brutal Bill would have brought home the bacon, and she would have been glad of it – she would. Bellowing bill would not have gone whining to his mum for the price of a fag and a tin.

Sighing she turned back to her boyfriend.

'Yeah or right io spus so.' They loped of down the road together.

From a distance they looked like scraps of paper, their manner of walking so listless, blown by the hurrying wind. Meanwhile, the dry leaves continued their aerial ballet, an upward spiral dance with the mad wind beneath the racing, furious clouds. It began to spit with rain.

Brella had a thick shock of raven hair that tore itself furiously away from the top of his forehead as if it were trying to escape from the force and weight of gravity. His skin was sallow, cheekbones high, lips generous and his teeth flashed ivory white and expensive each time he smiled. He was a charmer. He smiled often.

He was handsome in that curious English public school kind of way – and if it were not for his habitual shyness he would have been a ladies' man; and indeed, with the growing confidence of the coming years, this might, to be sure, prove to be the cut of it. His clothes were casual smart and one had to twice to realise that his taste was not only good but expensive.

He was post-post Thatcherite 'new man', and if his great-great-grandfather had suddenly appeared, unannounced from the ethereal drawing room on the other side of death there would have existed between them the easy rapport of mutual recognition. Two Edwardian dandies together who knew the meaning of life and the imperialism of pleasure, its bitch demands never satisfied.

In the Britain of the twenty-first century we had – through two world wars and a dying, ageing welfare state whose oxygen machine was about to be switched off by its arrogant and selfish children, in terms of political sense and social sensibility – come full circle. The common good was but a ream of austerity and affluence had not made the world kinder but sated and unconscious in its casual cruelty.

On Saturday nights, even in this small out of the way town. The streets were full of beggars(mostly bedraggled, maudlin and confused men) and the pretty girls tripping past would simply giggle and look the other way; or, if Brella was taking the air on his way to the local arts cinema, they would turn shy, furtive glances from under their fringes towards his slim direction.

Darwin or Christ? We were all, all of us, forever making that split-second choice. A certain French poet would have loved Brella; as the shop girls, trainee accountants and bank tellers would have loved him – but in a different way – had they had but the chance to breach his apparent inaccessibility had they realised that diffidence not detachment kept them at bay.

Another war? Computerised wars of the twenty-first century would isolate people from peoples and the consequence of their savagery, would not provide the visceral shock to awaken a sense of mutual wretchedness, our tired and transient, trudging footfall against history's long horizon.

All these elements, these wayward and listless thoughts of an idle moment, mystic and historic, that weak and watery autumn day conspired to induce a restlessness, an uneasiness and sense of disquiet beneath the blue/black shock of sleek wavy hair that flew from his forehead like a dead blackbirds wing that drifted and fell on the indifferent breeze. His body also, his corporal self, felt slightly queasy as he turned the corner and bowled his way to the local shop.

As he walked in, he saw a young girl, eighteen or twenty-two, standing, almost cowering in the corner by the newsstand, beneath the garish porno mags. He glimpsed her out of the corner of his eye and she flashed in his mind like the crosses, squares and numbers that used to flash before the start of old films. Consequently, his personal old film began to roll.

Years before – though not many years before – he had given a girl – a local girl whose mother worked in the kitchen at his school, his first adolescent crush poem. She was blonde, wide-faced and good looking, not like the waif in the corner, but nevertheless a connection between them had been made and the first words of the stanza bubbled into his mind like a bad toothache long forgotten.

'He shall be thy servant
And stand at thy door
And wait awhile
For the grace of your smile
And kisses nevermore.'

He inwardly winced at the clumsy sentimentality of his childish affections and the memory of the local yob who strode off with her one summer evening – her mocking smile, triumphant – looking back over her shoulder. He deeply resented the girl standing in the corner. She stared back at him with all the rancour of a starveling at a feast.

A copy of the Times, a carton of fruit juice and a small bag of apples under his arm, Brella waited patiently, if uncomfortably in the bright cheap atmosphere of the shop, in the queue at the cashiers.

In front of him a young man, cropped hair, curtain ring through his nose, shuffled ungainly towards the till.

'Twety Marlboro, pleas mate,' he sniffled – but his sniffle was like a grunt.

'Git twetty more Lee, Git twetty more will yer?' the girl under the porn mags shouted across the room.

'Twetty more mate,' said Lee pocketing the first packet.

The young female cashier gave him another packet from the shelf behind her and dropped the change on the counter after ringing the till twice. She was flustered under the hot, cheap lighting and confused by Lee's changing order.

'Wus this,' said Lee looking at his change.

'Oh sorry,' said the girl giving him the rest of his change. But it was too late.

'Yew fucken tryen to diddle me?'

Lee's eyes were full hatred – glistening with the dew of rage.

The girl stood back, 'No, no, I, I.'

She was visibly shocked and was beginning to shake.

'Yew fucken tryen a diddle ne yew fucken slag?'

'She fuken was Lee,' said Wendy – who was now by his side – snaking her arm through his. 'She fuken was.'

'I'll have yer yer fuken slag, I'll come through there and kick yer ribs in.'

The girl was shaking hard by now – her fat cheeks flushed with fear and the beginning of tears.

'Charming,' said Brella out loud – too loud – he thought he was talking to himself – after all he was no hero.

'She has n't bloody done anything. You are overreacting' said Brella amazed at his own levels of controlled contempt and anger that were flowing through his body, through his gritted teeth.

'For the grace of your smile,' streaked across his mind.

'C'mon, outside I'll fucken av yer.'

'I'm not going to fight with **you**.'

Brella was still amazed at his own steadfastness. There were people in the queue which made it easier for him to avoid respiration and retreat.

'Yes y'fucken are – I'll wait outside; yer comen outside?'

'Well of course I'm coming outside. What do you expect me to do? Hide behind the cornflakes?!'

A ripple of titters emerged from the crowd behind him.

'You lay one finger on me and I'll go to the police. There are witnesses here.'

The crowd became a bit restive.

'Well orioght. I'll be outside.' Lee's face was distorted with into folds of anger. 'Cunt' he said as he walked out the door – Wendy hanging on his arm. She looked back at him – her empty ashen face a sheet of pure rage, stunted hatred. (He shall be thy servant, And stand by thy door.)

Brella paid for his goods, and with some apprehension stepped outside. Thin little spots of rain were beginning to fall on the dirty pavement, on the empty street.

It was Sunday night a few days later and the autumn evening was darker than usual, blue/black clouds were banking up against the horizon and threatening thunder. An autumn gale was in the offering but Brella was in a good mood. His last day in this small town – his last day in Hicksville.

If it possible to say so there was a smile in his walk. He hummed along to a tune he just hears meandering from a nearby pen window. It was his father's favourite song – and one Brella normally hated – but nevertheless, it lodged like a nervous tick in his brain and he could not shake it off.

The falling introduction cranked away. Da da da da da dadle adle daaa.

'Imagine there's no heaven.'

The evening air was wet and heavy with the sweet/sour smell of rotting vegetation, which floated on the breeze like some unholy devotional incense. Brella inhaled deeply the heady aroma and noted the charcoal black branches beginning to nod sagely against the fading light.

'Yes indeed,' he said to himself with air of quiet self-satisfaction. Once again he felt pleased and energised by the essential rightness of things. Once again, his stride was confident, with just the hint of a swagger. A gentleman's swagger. It was his habitual evening stroll, however, he found himself in a part of the neighbourhood that was to him an unknown quantity. Unknown – and for that reason just a touch intriguing.

Swinging his arms in pseudo-military style, he turned into a narrow alley overlooked by swaying beech trees, their bony branches, like witches' fingers, scraping the top of the old brick wall that traversed the length of the narrow alley on the left side. As he walked down the wet flagstones he became aware of a series of inlets into small yards on the righthand side that opened and presented themselves to him. In the darkness they looked like giant cavities of pulled teeth in some hideous and filthy mouths.

In reality they were nothing more than scrappy backyards to the art deco style council flats and each dingy hole was populated by washing lines and overflowing communal dustbins which gave up their contents with an extravagant abandon which on any other context may have been confused with generosity. Filth as the extravagant charity of the poor.

'Yes indeed' he muttered to himself. 'Yes indeed. It's easy if you try.'

BUMFF.

'Shit – sorry mate.'

A hunched figure had torn out of one of the yards at twenty miles an hour and collided with Brella's confident, swinging gait and knocked him, in the narrow walkway, flat against the opposite wall.

'Shit – sorry mate,' the small hunched figure said once again. 'Are yew oroight?'

He peered up into Brella's astonished face. It had all happened so quick and Brella had no time to be fearful. As he stared down into the thin watery eyes, set like gravestones in the shaven skull, stretched over with dry, taught parchment like skin the dim light of mutual recognition began to dawn. The nose ring flashed gold light under the orange glow of glimmering street lights and Brella, had he been more self-aware, would have felt his heart rate increase.

Lee *felt* his heart begin to sink.

'Aw look mate. I'm really sorry what happened the other day. Oi was pissed off. Yew know how it is.'

Still peering, almost pleading, his watery eyes seemed now to be swimming in a bath of phosphorous orange, he presents his open flat hand in an act of reconciliation.

An old, stupid badly written childish poem flitted across Brella's mind as he firmly grabbed Lee's hand in an apparent act of acceptance.

In one swift unthinking movement Brella jerked Lee's hand downwards and smashed his forehead against the bridge of Lee's nose.

On the evening air, as indifferent as the clouds, the song continued, 'It's easy if you try.'

Stunned; Lee began to stagger backwards into the open pit of the back yard. Brella followed – punching and pushing and kicking as hard as he could as he felt a surge of relief flow through his system. Lee fell backwards between the two tall council dustbins; he crunched heavily against the rubbish that was wedged between the dustbins and which sprawled around their base.

There was the sound of cracking ribs and squelching splitting flesh as Brella kicked and kicked and kicked again the crumpled, shivering heap on the floor beneath him.

Lee was groaning and gasping between each swing of the leg and stamp of the boot, trying to raise himself up but never quite getting there.

In the distance –

'No hell beneath us- above us only sky.'

Brella stooped down and punched Lee full in the face five or six times. Lips were split, teeth were broken and blood spurted from his nose.

'Imagine all the people living for today.'

Groaning, but too stunned to speak, Lee was rolling amongst the rubbish and shit on the filthy gritty, asphalt ground. Brella stopped and took a look at the wheezing, spotting figure crumpled at his feet.

There was silence – apart from the old song – his father's favourite.

'You may say I'm a dreamer – but I'm not the only one.'

Lee tried to lift his face off the ground but the sticky blood and congealed snot was like fresh glue stretching and pulling in viscous strands in the narrow space between his face and the black tar of the grey asphalt. His lips were glued to the tar like an old squashed tomato. Bits of decrepit tabloid newspaper were blowing around his by now scarred and bloodied head.

Brella backed away slowly at first, breathing heavily with a curious sense of relief, he turned heel and quickly and confidently left the yard, brushing down his jacket and trousers.

With each round of Lee's laboured breathing, bubbles of snot and blood spluttered themselves on to the black ground oozed like piss into the pile of shit and rubbish, he empty Coke cans and fish finger packets; the used condoms, the social detritus, the collective stench of a disjointed community.

The lazy, languid limp-wrist lyrics lisped their final way to their final watery denouement

'I hope one day you'll join us,

And the world will be as one'

Whilst Lee spat blood and tree broken teeth into the cold wet asphalt.

Bubbles of blackening blood dribbled from Lee's mouth and congealed the broken teeth to the black floor as he tried to get up and crawl away, as he tried but failed to stand up, as he tried but failed to get onto his own two fuckin' feet

As Tristram Brella walked back – or rather fled way from the small yard into which he had inadvertently strayed – as he walked away from that scene in the now intensifying darkness – as he walked away from Lee's shuddering body– with his mind still stunned into paralysis by the unexpected strength of his own actions – the idea rather than the abstract thought 'the propaganda of the deed' floated into his mental vision. He did not feel the need to think but he felt strangely comforted by their semblance of reason – their hint of academic professorial approval. Was this the meaning of triumph was this the meaning of the phrase he had never understood – a good war?

Back in his small bedsitting room, which had rented for the last two weeks, he spread the Sundays out before him – all the quality Sundays – he saw himself – as free thinker – who could therefore think the unthinkable – and perhaps he had gone one step further – perhaps he had already done the unthinkable?

The room was solely lit by a one bar electric fire and small bedside lamp.

On the table bedside him, the waiting crumpets steamed contentedly on a small white plate. There was a cup of Earl Grey tea scented with a teaspoon of clear Peruvian honey. Two slices of lemon, sharp and bitter, floated and bobbed in the silky brown liquid.

Brella stretched out in the armchair and cupped his hands behind his head, gently cradling his skull. In the warm dark background the sound of Boccherini's Minuet in A major delicately danced in the darkness. Like glowing fire flies on summer evenings every nuance of sound seemed to illuminate his still aching and empty head.

Outside the autumn wind was banging an outhouse door. The gnarled trees, bent and rocked by the wind were scraping the fleeing clouds.

'Marvellous,' he thought. 'Bloody marvellous.'

Fall

If you should fall,
Would they catch you.
If your mask should suddenly slip.
If you should fall
Would they unlatch you
And cast you over hip from hip?

If you should fall,
Would they be there?
Would their beds be feather and down.
If you should fall.
Would they flee from there as all your eggs
Hit the stony ground,
Hit the stony ground.

You lost your ship,
Lost your moorings
Gave a shout in the nether world.
If you should slip.
Would they take the booking?
Help you out as your life unfurls
As your life unfurls.
If you should fall' would they be you?
Take your place
Come shining through?
If you should fall would they see you?
Or a face they never knew,
They never knew?

The Servant's Day

**'They had a touch of paradise,
a spell you can't explain
for in this crazy paradise,
They are in love with pain.'**

— 1 —

Jonathan the old servant (old that is in his spirit that is – not in years) stood rigidly to attention beside the front door. He was wearing a pair of thin and worn, black and baggy linen trousers (a 'gift' from his Mistress – a garment she had no more use for – it being now five years out of season); that hung loosely from his thin bony hips and flapped with an air of discordant and disconsolate resignation against his stick-like ankles of his bare and by now freezing feet. A white cotton collarless shirt, equally thin, equally threadbare hung from his shoulders with the same listless air of silent defeat.

It was five forty-five one late autumn afternoon and the servant was, as he always was at that hour of day, poised, waiting – waiting to open the door for his returning Mistress. His bare feet on the fashionable marble floor (champagne and flacked with salmon pink and emerald blue tiles) of his Mistress's stylish kitchen were now numb and almost blue with the cold.

Earlier that day, whilst he was serving Mistress her breakfast slave jonathan had made the foolish mistake of speaking out of turn. Or to be more precise – he had made the mistakes of not first signalling for permission to speak. That is, he had not placed his hands behind his back, knelt at her feet and pressed his forehead against the honey-yellow pine wood floor. (This of course was no guarantee of permission – very often Madam would ignore him – but at least it showed basic good manners.)

Indeed, good manners were one of Mistress Alexis's priorities in life; to be sure the Lady had a deep ingrained prejudice that good manners were of the very essence of life itself. The honourable Lady was therefore deeply shocked, if not hurt, that her servant should ignore this basic code of civilized and humane existence. And so Madam resolved there and then that if her underling should so choose to act like an animal he would therefore be treated as such and punished accordingly.

It was a cold, overcast day in late Autumn. Mistress Alexis, slave jonthnan's owner, was renowned for her wit and inventiveness in the manner of punishment and discipline of her staff – both domestic and commercial. The Madam had a genius for cruelty that was the envy and gossip of her contemporaries. Grey autumn clouds scudded by outside and dirty spats of rain began to tap tap splat on the kitchen window pane.

After this display of ill manners Madam slowly turned her face towards jonathan and, letting her large liquid brown, intelligent and penetrating eyes rest upon him for a good minute and a half, said, 'It is **very cold** today jonathan.'

Mistress turned back to her tea and, little finger crooked in the old fashion manner of studied gentility, sipped gently at the aromatic golden liquid. He did not reply. Indeed his Mistress would have counted it an impertinence if he had done so. As a slave it was universally agreed by all right-thinking people that his thoughts, opinions and feelings (should he have any?) were of no value. It was automatically assumed that the slave would and in reality must agree with his Mistress, who was indeed his social, intellectual and spiritual Superior.

He therefore did not, dare not speak.

Reflecting, almost wistfully, the Madam gazed in the middle distance.

'Yes, it is very cold today jonathan.' There was a slight pause. Madam was thinking. She said with a cold, sharp click of the cup on the china saucer, 'You shall wear no shoes.' Her tone was elated. A problem had been solved in a flash of intuition.

The sub clause of the sentence was given decisively, each separate word weighted with the force of moral law and the happiness of a judgement and sentence well-made and fitting.

Madam's house, as was the fashion, had no carpets – only highly polished floor boards and marble tiles throughout. The cruel significance of his Mistress's order was not lost on the slave. He took an inward gasp of air.

'But… but.'

'No buts jonathan' – she slapped his face. 'You shall wear no shoes today at all,' Mistress said again with a self-satisfied smile, seeing his obvious distress. She continued to gaze into the middle distance and delicately sip her tea. It was if she were speaking to herself; slave jonathan being no more than an irrelevant on-looker at the tragedy of his own existence, and not the sufferer and subject of her imperial commands.

Madam returned her attention to the breakfast table and began to nibble with the exquisite air of a refined gazelle on her toast and marmalade. All at once she stopped chewing and, meditatively, with her head slightly cocked on one side coughed delicately and said, 'Ahmm, you mayn't wear any underwear. You have behaved like a blundering beast this morning, spoilt my meditations, and, I may say so, given deep offence. Do beasts wear underwear? Do beasts wear shoes? They do not. Therefore you shall not wear shoes nor undergarments until further notice. Do beasts sit in chairs? No Theretofore you mayn't sit down until it please me to grant this privilege. Go to the toilet at the top of the house and change. Then you may come back and clear away the breakfast clutter and help me on with **my** shoes.' The Mistress smiled se-renely and arched her little finger even higher as she took another small sip of the warm and refreshing liquid. Slave jonathan turned quickly and quietly and, head-down, face burning with guilt – hands behind his back, padded softly out of the room.

That all happened this morning. All day, dressed in nothing more than thread bare linen trousers and a thin cotton shirt, slave jonathan had been about his quotidian tasks. The autumn wind whistled outside the house, and, although the central heating had been turned on an hour earlier in anticipation of his Mistress's return, after eight hours of domestic chores in the unheated house slave's feet were beginning to sting with the cold.

Nevertheless, still, like a good slave, like all good slaves should, jonathan awaited the return of his Mistress with eager anticipation. In spite of the cold that was keeping his legs, or perhaps, dear innocent reader, because of the cold that kept him shaking, shivering and frozen to the spot, save jonathan did not wish to move. Guilt stricken still, he had no desire to move. He did not wish to displease his Mistress by failing to open the door for her promptly upon her return.

And so he stood, legs shaking, feet turning blue and waited, And waited. And waited.

The sharp click, click and clack, like the sound of a wet whiplash against dry, naked skin, of expensive high heels on cold paving stones, the latter flecked with autumn leaves that were crushed quickly beneath her sole and instep with a dying almost grateful sigh, awakened the slave from his near frozen reverie. His Mistress was returning. His Mistress had\returned and the sound of her imperious stride, measured only by each resounding click and clack, click and clack, was the signal for her subject to assume the ritual position; dutifully he did so.

With the stiff mechanical movements of a clockwork toy; slave shuddered downwards onto his right knee. His head bowed, his left hand tucked ceremoniously behind his lower back, his outstretched right hand was poised expectantly on the catch of the door.

Click clack, click clack he listened to the sound he loved and counted each imperial step, as, with exquisite timing born of years of painful practise, slave jonathan slipped open the door and his Mistress strode in with not a break in her rhythm or hesitation in the onward flow of her confident gait. The Mistress, the owner of the being who was knelt in silent and pain-ridden adoration, flowed in and was herself a picture of poise, grace and elegance made manifest. She did not look at nor did she even greet her slave. In his turn jonathan was only allowed to gaze on his Mistress with her given consent. Consequently, as Madam made her entrance, slave could only glimpse the sharp points of his owner's fashionable court shoes. Could only hear the soft susurrations of silken thigh against silken thigh, could only smell the warm, dark aroma of Madam's pencil leather skirt as she almost floated past, with an air of blissful unconcern, within half an inch of slaves bowed and trembling head.

She did not look at nor did he greet her slave. It was indeed a matter of some amused contention between Madam herself and other colleagues, friends and slave keepers. As Madam often said when discussing the treatment of the social and the gender inferior, 'Does one greet one's cooker, one's washing machine. Does one address one's fridge or one's ironing board in the second person or by a proper noun?' (Madam had an MA in Linguistics – French, German and Spanish and was in the habit of making grammatical references.) 'No, one does not. Therefore why should one bother with one's servant other than to issues orders or deliver a reprimand?'

Just as Madam's spirit was universally noted and admired for its ruthlessness and cruelty, so was Madam's mind noted and also admired for it's no-nonsense clarity of purpose.

Mistress Alexis was in an expansive mood, expansive and luxurious. The Madam felt as expansive and as luxurious as the interior of her large, elegant rooms in her large elegant house. Standing in the middle of the polished floor (slave had been on his knees cleaning most of the afternoon) Madam surveyed all around her and took a deep breath in silent self-satisfaction. Mistress Alexis had had a good day. The clever businesswoman that she was had concluded two lucrative deals and, in front of several female members of staff had humiliated a male office junior. Over the two years that Madam had been head of department the Good Lady had perfected the art of verbal humiliation of her inferiors (or those who incurred her displeasure) almost to the level of a ritual art form. But Madam's art was no morbid meditation. Wit, humour and inventiveness were of the essence of her style and the four young girls on the reception desk had been entertained to the point of tears by the red-faced fumblings of the office junior under the verbal onslaught of Madam Alexis. (CEO MA.)

The Lady therefore felt well and felt well-pleased with the world as she slowly, one delicate finger at a time, removed first one snakeskin glove and then the other. Slave, after silently closing the door behind the object of his supine adoration, was standing, as he had been trained, at exactly five paces behind Madam. With slow, studied deliberation, Mistress Alexis neatly folded both gloves into her right hand. Madam then stretched out both arms at a thirty-degree angle to her body, arched the regal head backwards slowly and shook out her long auburn tresses – which fell dutifully below her shoulder line with the sound as of a skein of watered silk falling to a marble floor. This was slave's signal to remove her small bolero jacket. Holding his breath (Madam would not tolerate the feel of a domestic underling's breath upon her velvet and cream textured skin) slave stepped forward to complete this most important task, this first ritual of the early evening. With delicacy bordering on tender-ness, slave gingerly pinched the shoulder pads between first finger and thumb, as Madam gracefully swung her arms round to the parallel position behind her pointing towards him, and inching and shaking the precious garment(Madam was very particular about her 'things;' and this was a particularly expensive 'thing' from the house of Coco Chanel) slave gently slid it down her elegant, perfumed arms. To any outside observer this display would have seemed a sequence from a ballet, as indeed it was in the minutely choreographed protocol of slave and Mistress. To Madam this was nothing but good manners made concrete and his Mistress felt pleased that the hours of training and discipline she had lavished on her slave were beginning to bear fruit. Slave meanwhile could almost taste her feminine essence, feel the ambiance of her delicate scent as she shifted the coat from her shoulders.

His small reward furtively enjoyed he then scurried away, (he had the quick neurotic movements of a frightened discovered rodent that in his soul he had now become) with Madam's jacket and gloves to draw and hanger.

Mistress Alexis took the latest copy of *Vogue* from the magazine rack, and, on one elegant arabesque, folded herself into the black leather sofa. The surface of the leather was expensively cold and Madam gave a quick shudder of delight as she sank into its sucking, luxurious embrace.

After laying out Madam's clothes for the following morning (two sets – the ridding habit for Madam's Saturday morning ride and silk stockings, wool skirt, jacket and taffeta blouse for afternoon shopping and tea at Harrods), slave jonathan padded back into the lounge and stood, hands behind his back, head bowed, at the base of the sofa upon which Mistress Alexis was now reclining. He stood inches away from her outstretched feet. Paying no attention to him Madam languidly turned the heavy pages of the fashion magazine, her eye swimming slowly over the glossy surface. There was silence in the room for ten minutes. Slave stood, eyes cast down at an empty space on the floor and waited. The only sound was the sound of her breathing, the gentle flop of each turning page and the occasional creak of the sofa as, for more comfort, Madam shifted position. Without saying a word, but giving a very small cough ('emm') Madam raised her right foot. Slave immediately dropped to his knees. Cradling Madam's foot by the heel, slave, taking great care not to snag his owner's stockings, prised her foot from its expensive encasement. This done he placed the stiletto, with great reverence, beside the sofa. Madam then raised her other foot and the ritual 'de-shoeing' was repeated. The slave began to gently massage first one and then the other foot. He massaged using both thumbs rotating in clockwise and then again in anticlockwise movements – as he had been trained to do. This gave Madam maximum relief from the strains of the day. It was a technique Madam herself had taught slave and she always insisted he followed her teaching to the letter. Madam removed from the massaging hands and replaced the other for further treatment without prior warning. Madam crossed and uncrossed her ankles at will; as a result of which, in the course of twenty-five minutes, slave was caught off guard and kicked in the face at least five times. No matter. Madam continued to peruse her magazine unabashed. Like the Mona Lisa, a permanent smile, enigmatic, almost invisible, played around her full, sensuous lips – all at once Madam's smile became more pronounced. Madam shut the heavy magazine with a resounding smack and, in a maternal embrace of both folded arms pressed the magazine to her chest. She felt comforted by the feel of its cool silky pages against her soft skin, Madam's sense of pleasure increased as smiling to herself she said in a crisp English accent.

'Slave stop.'

Jonathan stooped immediately as he assumed the 'waiting for command position' (head bowed, hands clasped in the small of back) he remained kneeling. For few seconds Madam, head tilted slightly, gazed at him with evident satisfaction. 'You may continue the massage with your mouth and tongue.'

Slave obeyed. Apparently unconcerned Madam returned to her magazine. As part-punishment for his morning clumsiness Madam had restricted slave to one half tumble of water. And full well she knew that he would be fully parched and his mouth and tongue would be extremely dry by now. Her smile increased and her sense of fun was awakened as she felt his stiff lips and unresponsive tongue struggle to cope with the task he had been set.

'Slave stop,' Madam said; rather sharply this time as if she had been annoyed. 'Go to the kitchen and fetch the carafe of orange juice from the fridge.'

Quickly, and with anticipation, slave padded, almost ran to the fridge. Thinking Madam intended to relieve his thirst and moisten his lips for the purpose of a more efficient massage slave returned with the juice and two tumblers on a silver slaver.

He placed the salver on the small table beside the sofa, poured a glass of juice and handed it to his Mistress. Without raising her eyes from the magazine and with an extended little finger Madam took the glass from him and continued reading. As she took the first sip Madam glanced upwards and caught sight of slave still standing by the sofa.

In mock surprise, for she was secretly pleased her ruse was unfolding to plan, Madam batted her eyelids.

'What are you waiting for, spittleflim (her pet name for him when she was angry) finish the massage.'

Slave turned to go but Madam said with great emphasis – the word sounding like a sharp crack.

'Stop.' The word sounded sharp and quick – like gunfire.

'What is this?' Madam held the spare tumbler aloft. She shook it backwards and forwards quickly in front of his face accusingly… 'What is this?'

'I told you to get one glass and you bring two tumblers. Take this back to the kitchen wash it, dry it, and place it in the cupboard where it belongs. Then return here and kneel beside me'

Slave bowed in obedience and repentance and, tumbler in hand did as he was bidden. He returned quickly, hands behind his back, and knelt beside her. His eyes as always were fixed upon the floor. Madam ignored him for some minutes as she continued reading. Presently Madam shut the magazine and handed it to slave.

'Replace this in the rack and give me the *Woman's Home Journal.*'

Slave took the magazine, stood up, put the magazine in the rack (which was actually just beside the sofa and well within Madam's reach) and gave his mistress that month's edition of the *Woman's Home Journal.*

He returned to his kneeling position. Madam laid the magazine across her knees and sighed.

'Look at me jonathan.'

Slave raised his eyes to meet hers. Large liquid pools of milky brown chocolate, glistening in an almond of blue veined marble; in the fading evening twilight, they twinkled with merry amusement and seemed, at that moment, to be the only source of light.

They were like two candles in a dark window on winter evening. They glistened with delight and a touch of merry malevolence.

Slave felt himself melting inside, as if his soul was being subsumed under Madam's steady and all-consuming gaze. He could not hold the look and let his head drop. Madam took his chin between her thumb and first finger and, with almost maternal solicitude (almost but not quite) raised his head to revisit her unfailing gaze.

'Look at me jonathan.'

Her grip was firm and in any case, slave dare not struggle. Once again he felt his very essence, that feeble sense of manly selfhood, so dearly won through past millennia of striving and usually maintained, in the distant and now outlawed and forbidden past, by periodic outbursts of threatening violence, he felt once again, the shreds of his essence and all sense of self dissolve under her powerful and, it had to be admitted, voluptuous gaze.

Her liquid gaze was turning everything to water.

'Look at me jonathan.'

jonathan looked as he was bidden, and, despite his cold, the hard wood freezing his knees, despite his thirst and hunger, he felt a deep, dark warmth, the colour of purple and damask, flooding every inch of his inner being. The reward for this surrender, the non-payable price of his defeat was this peculiar perversion, this almost pleasure, a kind of stultified peace.

'Look at me.'

Madam smiled

'Close your eyes and remain in that position.'

Madam returned to her magazine. Slave, now that he was no longer the object of her attention, was in utter darkness; the warmth he felt under her gaze only a moment ago was slowly seeping away and the full effect of the cold, the icy floor boards, the eight hours with no food, the continual work, was beginning to have its effect. As Madam continued to leisurely flick page after page of the *Woman's Home Journal* slave began, in silence, involuntarily to shiver. On the sofa Madam moved and stretched and resettled herself for greater comfort and felt the tension of the day slowly slip away.

'MMM.' Madam hummed to herself as she settled into the now warm embrace of the soft leather.

Behind closed eyes, shivering with cold, in his darkness jonathan could here no sound in the large elegant room save the soft plop of each turning page, the tick of an antique clock Madam had purchased in Paris, and the soft susurration of a silk blouse against flesh theta kept pace with Madam's rhythmic contented breathing.

Outside, the scudding clouds began gathering in the darkness. Time ticked by. Twenty minutes, thirty minutes, Ignoring her slave, Madam continued reading.

Nothing but silence. The soft susurration of moving silk. In the darkness slave shivered. He could hear his Mistress breathing and smell her delicate rose fragrance. Time ticked by. Nothing but silence, darkness and cold inside his lonely skull. His legs and torso were now shaking with the cold. His knees were aching with stiffness. A slight creak of leather. The flop of the closed magazine on Madam's lap. The soft click of the clock ticked down the darkening evening.

In her spare time, of which Madam enjoyed an extraordinary amount, Madam was a keen and accomplished tennis player. And so it was that with her outstretched, elegant manicured hands, nails of deep autumnal russet, Madam leaned over slightly and as if delivering an opening volley slapped slaves face as hard as she could and on the backward swing Madam then slapped the other cheek with her reversed palm as hard as she could, with all the lust drive force of malevolent pleasure madam could muster; and although he was expecting punishment, the severity of Madam's 'service' took slave completely, unnaturally, by surprise. Despite himself, his stoical delusions, slave's bright crimson cheeks began swimming with salt water. Madam took his cheek between her forefinger and thumb.

'Open your eyes, look at me.'

Through bleary eyes slave saw Madam Alexis's merry and inquisitive eyes.

'Do not presume to indulge yourself in disobedience jonathan. Now you may prepare the evening meal.'

Silently, slave jonathan rose and repaired to the kitchen.

Madam returned to her magazine article:
'The Care and Discipline of Domestic Staff and The Gender Challenged' by Lady Estrela Brand Phd. Msc.

— 2 —

Lady Kathleen Maria Estrela Brand was of sterling and stern Scottish Andalusian decent.

The lady's regal manner commanded instant respect amongst her social equals and trembling awe amongst those of her social inferiors foolish or unlucky enough to cross her imperial path. They were like rowing boats nudged by the bows and caught in the slip stream of a blousy ocean liner. In her wake lay the bodies of her discarded lovers and the broken souls of her willing slaves. The Lady habitually wore her dark raven hair tied up in a stiff little bun at the top of her head; crowned and held in place by a silken rose of the purist white and the most exquisite feminine delicacy. This in turn was pierced by an elegant silver-plated hairpin topped by a small spherical hand grip of purest gold. At times he wore a pair of black horn-rimmed spectacles that gave her, not uncharitably, an air of serious and intellectual intent. Lady Kathleen was serious; yes, bookish, yes, but she also fully embraced the sensual pleasures of a well-balanced bourgeois life. She was no austere blue-stocking. Indeed, she saved her austerity for her inferiors, (which in truth, was where it served to good effect.) The head of Madam Alexis's department was blessed with high intelligence and possessed s creative and passionate nature. Kathleen Maria Estrela-Brand was, in every sense of the term – cultured, confident capable – a being in short of Superior quality. And that evening, unbeknown to jonathan, shivering at his kitchen task, the Great Lady was coming to dinner.

Summoning her slave by gently ringing the small hand bell Madam kept for this purpose on the tiny coffee table beside the sofa – Lady Alexis raised her eyes rather sharply towards her servant as, wringing his has on an old dishcloth, he padded through the kitchen door.

'I know this is the last Friday of the month and I know it is short notice and I make no apology but you will not be dining with me this evening as is the custom I am afraid.'

The Mistress hesitated for a moment as she registered the expression of pained disappointment on her servant's face. (According to the most fashionable theories allowing the gender challenged the occasional taste of civilised life was good household management technique; and slave jonathan, for his part, looked forward to his monthly treat. His disappointment was, therefore all the more poignant.)

Madam smiled sweetly and continued. 'The Director of my Company is coming to dinner and because it I such short notice there is nothing for it but that Lady Bran is to have your portion for this evening. You are to serve at table. You may of course, have the scraps.'

Waving him away back to his tasks with the back of her hand Mistress Alexis languidly returned to her magazine. Smiling to herself, her head tilted slightly to one side as she continued her article. Madam said in a voice just loud enough for her retreating servant to hear, 'Always supposing there are scraps of course.'

A quick tingle of pleasure raced up Madam's spine and down again like a small electric shock. She shivered and shook herself.

The clock whirred up and gently struck seven. Silence, like milk being poured into an empty jug, re-flooded the house.

Another leisurely page was turned.

Slave jonathan trembled at his tasks in the cold kitchen and felt, somewhere between his hungry ribs, the sensation of his spirit melting and a warmness, like the rush of an anaesthetic or the firsts flush of whisky, nuzzle itself beneath purple with cold goose-pimple skin.

Weak with tiredness, it was when he was basting the sea bass with white wine that slave smelt the soft rose fragrance and warm breath of Mistress Alexis close to his left shoulder. Between finger and thumb Madam firmly clasped his lower earlobe, the side of her russet nails digging sharply into the soft flesh, slave winced as Madam pulled his head round level with her smouldering eyes. The Mistress, seething with intensity, held his gaze for a moment and pulled up fiercely on the earlobe when he tried to lower his gaze from the arch of her penetrating vision. Slave's face grimaced with pain as Madam tightened her grip, a small drop of blood began to appear round the corner of the elegant thumbnail. Almost hissing between gritted teeth Madam said – carefully enunciating each word *'You will not let me down this evening jonathan.'*

Still the Mistress held his gaze for a few seconds and then her expression softened to warm smile. Letting go of his ear quickly (the relief as painful as Madam's grip) the Mistress turned to the sink and, with a look on her face that said 'bad smell', Madam washed away the slave's blood under splashing cold water.

Lady Kathleen Maria Estrela Brand had come straight from a business meeting. The erudite lady had not had time to change for the evening's entertainments but was comfortably turned out in a chic linen and silk coal black business suit. The three-quarter length pencil skirt settled gently just above the near perfect round of Madam's near perfect knees encased in smoke grey stockings and the smart tailored jacket with Nehru collar hung gracefully from her shoulders. It caressed her figure with an almost military precision. The overall effect was neat, clean, sharp and breath-taking in its economy, simplicity and elegance.

Against the inclement inclination of the season Madam topped the suit with a high collard overcoat of thick wool charcoal grey picked out in a subtle dogtooth design. She wore high heel court shoes topped by a small red silk bow near the sharp pointed toe. Under her jacket was a small waistcoat beneath which rustled softly white ivory blouse of crushed silk. Perfumed by Chanel Madam clutched a thin document case of the finest black leather.

Instructing her driver to wait Lady Brand strolled up the path towards the house of Madam Alexis and was surprised, delighted and amused when, two steps from the entrance, the front door, as if by magic, opened for her. Madam sailed in and with only a quick glance at the kneeling figure clutching the door knob, laughingly greeted her friend and colleague.

'Darling Alexis, how marvellous of you to arrange such a perfect entrance. You simply must tell me,' she said, casting over her shoulder a look of amused contempt at the figure of jonathan as he now struggled to his feet, 'you simply must tell me your training methods.'

They kissed each other on the cheek four times and then stood looking at each with rapt mutual admiration.

'Welcome Lady Brand it is so lovely to see you.'

'Ahmm,' there was a small cough behind Lady Brand.

'Oh' said Mistress Alexis, awakened from her reverie.

'Slave jonathan wants to take your coat.'

'Of course,' said Maria Brand, still smiling at Alexis as she stretched out her arms behind her. In one expert movement slave lifted the overcoat from her shoulder and slid the garment deftly down her arms. There was a soft swish of silk on flesh. She instinctively shook her hair loose from the high collar.

Slave waited as Madam Brand handed him her leather gloves. As he padded away to store the clothes in the wardrobe Lady brand said: 'You are to be congratulated in your servant, having such a useful piece of equipment must by very satisfying.'

'Thank you Lady Brand, you are too kind, but one does one's best,' Madam Alexis beamed. Suddenly her face darkened and her eyes narrowed as her servant padded back through the room on his way to the unfinished tasks in the kitchen.

'You may bring the wine now, the Rioja '67.' Her sharp order like the slash of a knife through silk.

While he was fishing about in the back kitchen, he could hear the soft warm mummer of their conversation; their laughter sparkling up at irregular moments like Christmas twinkling tree lights.

As he padded softly back into the room with the silver serving tray, the Grigio '67 and two large wine glasses the air seemed magically drained of warmth as the two women eyed him coldly. Their conversation ceased. Jonathan placed the tray on the small table, uncorked and poured the wine. He handed first a glass to Lady Brand and then one to his Mistress. An enigmatic, disdainful smile played around Madam's Brand's lips as she took the glass. But the servant kept his eyes cast downwards and did not catch the sardonic twinkle in her eye.

'Thank you, servant,' her voice rang clear with ice-cold formality.

Madam Alexis too the glass from her slave and motioned him back to the kitchen with a wave of her hand.

The warmth of pleasant conversation continued. Lady Brand lent back in her chair, luxuriously exhaled a long trail of blue smoke. 'Darling, you really must see the Fendi collection this season. I was I Paris last month and his furs are absolutely divine.'

'Yes, I recently read the same in *Vogue*. Silk and fur are my favourite fabrics – they make one feel so, so…'

Madam Alexis searched for her word.

'Powerful,' Lady Brand interjected helpfully.

'Yes – that's the word' Madam Alexis eye were shimmering with light.

'Powerful and sensual.'

'My dear,' said Lady Brand gently touching Madam Alexis on her black stockinged knee.

'My dear, they are different words meaning the same thing,' and they both broke into gently but ringing laughter.

In the cold back kitchen, the slave was putting the last touches to the evening meal; in the darkness of his mind the Christmas lights began to twinkle.

As the mirth subside and the warmth of the wine bean to take affect Madam Alexis said.

'As a matter of fact, I intend to take a two-week vacation in Paris as soon as the Company can spare my services.'

Once again Lady Brand laid a reassuring hand on Madam Alexis knee.

'Darling you do not have to ask. You have my permission and blessing. Indeed, the Fendi collection is such a delight it would be a crime to miss it. In fact I positively order you to go.'

'Thank you Lady Brand,' said Alexis, bowing her head in mock humility. 'I am always your obedient servant.'

The mutual laughter tinkled on the air, spilling like silver mercury through the evening.

'Speaking of servants, your training methods will be in high demand when the Ladies of Parisian Society observe your slave's alacrity in questions of obedience and service.'

'Oh I shall not take him.'

'Oh?' Lady Brand's eyebrows were raised slightly. 'Then what is to be done with him?'

'I will leave him here. Locked in. It is for his own good – so he will come to no harm.'

'Here? Locked in? Will he like that?'

'I have absolutely no idea,' Madam Alexis said. 'There was a look of surprise on her face. And then quizzically – 'Does it matter?'

'Oh absolutely not' said lady Brand waving her cigarette dismissively.

In mutual recognition and understanding the two ladies, relaxing, one on her sofa and the other in her chair, beamed at each other.

There was a brief hiatus of silence.

'Well, would you care to eat? Slave is an excellent cook.'

'Rather,' said Lady Brand. It does smell very mouth-watering.'

Madam Alexis stood up, smoothed down her pencil leather skirt, her tone and expression changing from warm to cold, from soft to severe in an instant, commanded in sharp clear but modulated tones.

'Spittleflim, slave, you will serve dinner upstairs immediately.'

It was just as Lady Brand and Alexis arrived at the bottom of the stairs when they were stopped by the pummelling sound of feet on hard wood as slave trundled quickly into the living room. With a violence that surprised and almost frightened Madam Alexis; slave. hands clasped behind his back in accordance with protocol, threw himself into the 'begging for permission to speak' position.

Almost simultaneously his knees and forehead cracked against the hard wood floor.

'What is this?' Lady Brands face wore a mask of shocked amusement.

'It is nothing, My Lady, the little servant is being silly, He wants permission to speak, it is no matter. We can ignore him.'

'No perhaps not,' said Lady Brand, her fingers pressed together in a 'church steeple' tapping musingly against full, moist, crimson and slightly parted lips. 'He does right to ask, if it is not too much trouble, it would be amusing and indeed instructive to hear his voice. The voice, like the eye, is, after all, the key to the inner spirit.'

Madam Alexis, keen to please her guest immediately changed her position.

'Yes of course Lady Brand. You are right. Perhaps you would like to give the order yourself?'

'That would indeed be a pleasure.'

Lady Brand folded her arms across her midriff, lifted her head high and, looking down the ridge of her nose at the supine figure softly commanded. 'Well, speak servant. You have one minute. Not a second longer.' Out of the corner of her eye Lady Brand glanced and smiled at Madam Alexis. Madam Alexis smiled back. The silken bonds of mutual recognition, admiration were growing stronger by the minute.

Slave jonathan began to raise his head. Immediately Madam Alexis placed the pointed toe of her court shoe on his head and firmly pressed down. Slave's forehead, for the second time that evening, hit the floor with a dull crack.

'You mayn't look at us spittlefilm' said the Madam, her face cold with thunder.

'Quite right,' said Lady Brand approvingly. 'Speak servant.'

From the head squashed against the floor, (Madam Alexis was slowly increasing the pressure to encourage her slave too hurry up) a thin mouse like voice began to utter, 'Please Mistress Katherine, Mistress Ale…'

'Speak up idiot we are not straining our ears foe you.'

'Please Mistress Katherine, Mistress Alexis, I have not had time to set the table yet…' shouted jonathan in desperation.

At this unwelcome news Madam Alexie pressed her foot down even harder upon slave's head. Jonathan felt his nose and lips pressing deep into the cold wood floor and his teeth began to cut hard against his inner lip.

Giving one last exasperated push of her foot, Madam released slave's head from the pressure. 'Well, set it then, spittelflim idiot **NOW**.'

Slave shuffled his way to his feet, bowed quickly to both Ladies and ran upstairs to complete Madam's orders.

'I am so sorry Lady Brand. He will be punished presently.'

'It is no matter. As it is you did very well.'

'Thank you so much. Would you care for a glass of wine?'

'That would be an excellent idea.'

In the hush of the warm evening, they resettled themselves, together this time, their knees touching, on the black leather sofa.

— 3 —

The six black candles, bedded snuggly in two antique silver candelabras, emitted long flames of crimson/gold which, in concourse with the reddish light from the open fire, cast deep and dancing shadows round the room, the pictures, the antiques, the tapestries, the Chinese ceramics and the heavy mahogany furniture. Scented, their smoke was like an obscure but persistent incense.

The two ladies sat at either end of the long mahogany table. Their conversation, as ever, was light bantering, full of mutual congratulation. Their laughter, in the cluttering light was like the sparkling of diamonds in an ancient cavern or a coal-black vault.

As punishment for his earlies failings, slave jonathan was standing in the farthest, darkest and coldest corner of the room with his hands on his head.

Lady Brand was renowned for her sense of fun and the silver sounding laughter was subsiding from another cruel but elegant witticism.

'I said to Paul, the office auxiliary, failing your account-ancy exams once may look like a mere misfortune, but failing them twice – the is simply clumsy carelessness. But then again I do rather think the terms male and clumsy are interchangeable. A bit like the word stupid – don't you think? The little creature looked like a hurt and startled rabbit caught in the head lights. Could not, dare not say a thing.'

'Well rather like your junior this morning. I don't think we will be hearing much from that particular quarter for a while.'

The wine glass was three inches away from Lady Brand's perfumed arm, outstretched along the pure white table linen.

The two women gazed at each other down the long table. There was silence. Madam Alexis rang the small hand bell. It's sound tinkled and sparkled like a fairy light in the overwhelm-ing darkness.

Quickly, quietly, hands behind his back the slave arrived at Madam Alexis's side.

Still gazing at Lady Brand Alexis asked, 'Would you care for another glass of wine?'

'That would be wonderful – then I simply must go.'

Without looking at jonathan, Madam Alexis said, 'Pour Lady Brand another glass of wine servant.'

It had been a long day, the servant was tired, cold and his legs and arms were aching as he carried the bottle down to where Lady Brand was waiting.

The two Ladies continued gazing with rapt attention at each other for a while and then Lady Brand, lifting her head slightly, let her attention rest dreamily – somewhere in the mid-dle distance.

The servant softly clinked the bottle on the edge of the glass as the rich red liquid plopped into its elegant embrace. Still meditating on the middle distance, languidly, with the luxuri-ous slowness of aristocratic self-assurance and reserve, Lady Kathleen Maria Estrela Brand PhD abstractly reached for her glass. Slave had not quite finished pouring. He was tired and finding it difficult to focus. The was a confusion of bottle, glass and delicate manicured hand as the wine glass slipped on the white linen, the liquid oozing out like a bloody red wound on the pure white cloth, rolled off the table edge and smashed into jagged shards on the hard wood floor. The splinters glinted coldly in the yellow candle light.

Snapping from her reverie, Lady Brand pushed back her chair, stood up, and in one clean and practised stroke slapped jonathan hard in the face.

'You clumsy little cretin, you have split wine on my skirt.'

'I am sorry Madam, but you knocked the glass.'

The stunned silence was as loud as violent thunder. The two women gave each other a knowing look; like two musicians long used to playing together, an intuitive understanding was beginning to grow between them. The silken threads of an unholy bondage were beginning to oh so slowly tighten. No sound in the room save the gentle grackle of the fire and the hiss of six black candles.

Quickly picking up a serviette, slave knelt at Madam Brand's feet and began dabbing nervously at the red stain.

'I'm very sorry Madam, most very sorry Madam,' the slave stammered.

Regaining her composure Lady Brand laid her hand gently on the servant's head.

With infinite softness she murmured, 'Be quiet, be quiet.' Her voice was like gentle rainfall, soothing and hypnotic and slave began to cry inwardly as he was overtaken by an unexpected wave of tenderness.

Stroking his head as slave tried sans success to remove the stain allowed her fingernail to gently slide down his cheek as she presented the back of her hand for him to kiss. He kissed the hand once; then she offered her palm for the same salutation. Accepting his second homage Lady Brand cupped his cheek in her hand and gently stroked the side of his face with her thumb. Lady Brand tilted his face upward and stared into his eyes.

'I am not your Mistress. You do not have to apologise to me. You should apologize to your Mistress for letting her down and spoiling her evening. Go to her now.'

Jonathan began to get to his feet but Lady Brand laid an imperious finger on his head and pushing him down said softly.

'No, stay on your knees – the kneeing walk will do you good. Go straight to her.'

The thin shards of glass lay scattered on the floor between the servant and Madam Alexis. He looked up imploringly at Lady Brand's handsome face. The fine Lady had her arms folded no-nonsense Matron style across her bosom. Her head was cocked on one side and her eyebrows raised in an air of surprised enquiry.

'Is there a problem?' The slave looked terrified at the glass.

Lady Brand leaned over the quivering servant. She brought her face very close to his. Their eyes met in a magnetic clinch.

'There is no problem, jonathan. You must think positively. Walk carefully – any pain you suffer on account of the glass will simply be yours, and I may say very much deserved, bad karma for spoiling your Mistress's evening and ruining my perfectly good skirt.' Her voice, formerly warm and nurturing, was suddenly laced with ice as she added. 'By rights it she be taken out of your wages – but you are not even good enough to earn wages – are you **SERVANT**?!'

Lady Brand pulled herself up to her full height, extended her arm down the full length of the old table.

'Go,' she said quietly and firmly 'and let us have no more of your nonsense.'

'Yes, come to me slave, said Madam Alexis from the far end of the table. 'Come to me.' His Mistress crooked her finger. Her face was beaming with pleasure at Lady Brand's command of the situation.

Gingerly slave put one foot/knee in front of the other as he tried in vain to miss the broken glass scattered on the floor before him. Wincing as each little splint entered his knee, shin and toes, slave finally arrived at the feet of his Mistress. She was leaning back languorously, one arm supported on the back of the chair, the other resting quietly on the cool linen tabletop. There was a long cigarette holder in her left hand. As jonathan knelt at her feet Alexis grabbed her slave by the hair, yanked back his head, leaned over him and blew a long hot steam of smoke into his face.

'Darling Alexis,' said Madam Brand from the other end of the table. 'I think it might be useful if I take notes. I may pick up tips for my next article in the *Journal*. If you would wait a second while I fetch my notebook from downstairs. It is in my document case.'

'Yes of course. No matter. My servant will fetch it for you. Slave – go downstairs and fetch Madam's document case. Be quick about it.'

The Mistress let go of his hair and jonathan struggled to his feet wincing the while as the shards of glass began to bite into his thin cold flesh.

Once down stairs slave rushed into the kitchen and pulled a pair of tweezers from the first aid box and deftly removed as many splinters as possible. Returning through the living room he snatched up the slim leather case and ran upstairs.

Lady Maria Brand had removed herself next to Alexis on order to observe the 'ritual of discipline' more closely. She sat with her knees slightly together and her hands folded demurely across the taut fabric of her skirt. Slave sunk to his knees, head bowed in submission, and, with the case elegantly balanced upon outstretched palms offered Mistress brand her property. It shimmered darkly in the candle light.

'Stay in position.' The soft sensual voice of Lady brand weighed heavy on slave's tired ears. The near dead weight of authority.

Mistress brand snapped open the thin cases and realigned it as if slave's hands were nothing more than the leaf of a writing table. His hands began to waver with fatigue.

'KEEP STILL SPITTLEFILM.' Madam Alexis voice rapped out sharply like the sound of breaking icicles.

With studied efficiency Lady Brand quickly withdrew her pen and notepad. The case was snapped shut deftly but with such force that slave began to buckle slightly, his cut knees smarting on the hard wooden floor.

'Ahhh,' slave let slip in spite of his best efforts; but neither Lady Brand nor Mistress Alexis took a blind rat's spit of notice.

'You may place the case on the table,' said Madam Brand as she crossed her legs, flipped open her notepad and rested it on the angled bulge of her now repositioned, ample but elegant thigh.

The table was one inch away from where she was stationed. Slave took the document case. Stood up and let it plop softly on the dark wood. He was half way down to his kneeling position when Lady Brand said, 'Stop. Realign the case correctly. At right angles to the edge of the table. I cannot abide sloppiness.'

His knees still hurt, his back stiff, slave straightened up and did as he was commanded. As soon as the servant was on his knees once again Lady Brand said to Alexis.

'Well, my dear, I think we can begin the punishment. At the very least it will be the perfect end to a near (here her eyes narrowed as she looked down at the servant) perfect evening.'

'Quite right,' said Mistress Alexis as she affixed a cigarette into the long holder. Madam Alexis looked down at slave.

'Look up at me servant and open your eyes and mouth.'

Jonathan jerked his head up with alacrity. He was pleased to be able to gaze upon his Mistress for a few moments.

Madam smiled down at her underling and slowly put to end of the holder into her mouth closing her lips slowly and seductively round the stem. All the while she was smiling ruefully at her slave. Mistress slightly parted her lips several times, gripping the stem with her teeth she wrapped her lips around the black mouthpiece, letting the stem slide slowly in and out, in and out of her wet and glistening lips. Still smiling, a soft knowing smile as she leant over and grabbed her servant by the hair and pulled back his head as hard and as far back as she could. Jonathan felt as if his neck were about to break. Madam Alexis sucked heavily and deeply on the stem of the holder. She brought her lips very, very close to his and puckered her lips as if she were about to kiss him. Sparkling demons were dancing merrily in her dark eyes. Mistress knew, as she knew everything about her slave, that jonathan could not smoke and moreover had weak delicate lungs. From deep within her diaphragm Madam blew thick pungent smoke out into her slave's mouth and down, down into his diseased airways. His Mistress was so close to him that he could smell the sweet scent of her ruby lips, the faint aroma of her face powder and was grateful for the nearness of her femininity, almost like intimacy, almost a loving gift as he began to cough and splutter and choke on the acrid poison with which she was infecting him. He struggled and pulled back, trying to wrench his head to left and right and back away; but Madam was strong as with only one hand she held her slave to the sticking post. She chuckled warmly to herself as she sucked again on the holder and blew more of the white-blue smoke into his struggling mouth.

In his panic and confusion slave jonathan heard Lady Brand take a deep breath. She was full of surprise and admiration at Alexis skill and cunning in the art of discipline. The in-rush of air sounded like sea water swishing over rocks or the passing of fine silk over clean fresh skin. It sounded far way; music from another shore.

Slave was struggling and spluttering, attempting to raise himself – his feet and knees knocking and hammering on the cold floor.

Again Mistress Alexis puffed on the elegant holder and held her captive fast. To Lady Brand, who was a keen aficionado of blood sports, he reminded her of the Spanish bulls I the entrance to the bullring being prodded and stabbed by the picadors into anger and panic prior to their almost certain death.

Like them, no matter how much he railed he could not free himself from the power and cunning of a superior intelligence. The invisible might of a superior mind tormenting the lower beasts.

Lady Brand muttered almost inaudibly, 'My dear.'

Still holding her slave by his hair Madam slackened off and sat back to admire her handiwork. She let his head fall forward slightly; for a few moments she was loosening the leash.

Mistress Alexis sighed contentedly, took another luxurious draft on the stem and let the smoke float upwards into the middle air. At the breakfast table that morning (a time which seemed to jonathan, in his present torment, from another century) Madam Alexis's expression was abstract, lost in meditation. Now she was more focused.

From the metaphysical realm known only to the practitioners of her select and esoteric form of mediation his Mistress returned to the task she had set herself- the demonstration being given for the edification and entertainment of Lady Brand.

Pulling on his hair Madam gently forced back his head to its former near neck-breaking position. She brought her lips very close to his eyes.

'Close your eyes jonathan,' she said softly. Close your eyes jonathan' her voice like an invocation, a prayer, said again and again three times.

The slave as still trying to breath, to recover his equilibrium – in turns he was sputtering and coughing.

'Come on, for me, for your Mistress, close your eyes jonathan.'

Like the good slave he so wanted to be, the child so desperate to please; jonathan did as he was asked.

Her lips were now very close to his eyelids. He could feel her soft breath on his face, smell the faint whiff of her expensive scent. Her silk blouse was brushing gently against his cheek as she kissed first one then the other of his eyes.

There was a hush in the room as of a church service or some other spiritual event; as of the reverence before a Christening or the solemnity of a funeral. The ambience was difficult to define and hard to defeat and Lady Brand could not withstand its insidious imperatives.

'Excellent,' Lady Brand said to herself in sotto voce tones full of breathless respect and admiration.

'Excellent... excellent,'

In her perfect shorthand she made rapid notes.

As slave felt the wet kisses on his closed eyelids the warmth of her breath and aroma from her skin sent him off into delicious reverie. Her wholly premeditated token of tenderness touched him to the core. The caress of her lips and the touch of her hand was opium to his pain; trembling his insides began to melt.

Using her first finger and thumb Madam Alexis pulled open his left eyelid. Automatically slave's other eyelid flickered awake.

'No,' Alexis scolded, 'keep your right eye closed for the moment servant.'

The Mistress chuckled darkly as she placed the hot tip of her cigarette within a few centimetres of jonathan's now terrified eye. He pulled away sharply. Without saying a word Lady Brand laced her notepad and case on the table, stood up and resting her cool hands on his shoulders straddled the slave from behind. He squirmed and struggled as his head pushed heavily against the taut fabric of Madam's skirt stretched tightly across her upper thighs. His head rested in the V of her womanhood. Like Madam Alexis – Lady Brand was a keen athlete and using her ample strength effortlessly he pushed jonathan's face back towards the glowing tip of his Mistress's cigarette. Slave closed his eyes tightly and as Madam Alexis took another draw on the elegant holder he could feel the increased heat warming through his closed lids. Madam quickly swung the cigarette away from the screwed-up face, pulled open his eyelid and blew the hot acrid smoke into the centre of his pupil. Lady Brand had her right hand on his head. As he struggled and cried as she stroked his forehead like a mother with a fractious and frightened child at his first inoculation.

It was getting late so Mistress Alexis deftly pulled open his left eyelid and repeated the operation. in the acrid smoke – both eyes began to swim with stinging tears. Mistress Alexis sat back in her chair and Lady Brand returned to her notepad. Despite his distress, instinctively slave assumed the waiting for an order position. Kneeling. Hand clasped behind his back, head down, his eye burning.

'There,' said Madam Alexis with a satisfied sigh. 'All over. In case you're wondering slave, the smoke in the eyes was for the spilt wine; to teach you to look what you are doing in future, the mouth treatment was to teach you not to speak out of turn as you did at breakfast this, or rather now, yesterday morning. You may clear away the dishes. You may have my leftovers for your repast. You are certainly not eating Lady Brand's. They are far too good for you. Now go and be about your duties, servant.'

So saying the Mistress smiled sweetly and rested her clasped hands in her neat lap. Save obeyed and padded silently down stairs, the dishes and wine glasses placed ceremoniously on an old tray.

'Well,' said Lady Brand when the servant was out of earshot. 'You certainly have an interesting technique I must say. It is an old principle, the mixing of the hope of pleasure, the possibility of tenderness with the fear of pain. I'll admit that you have a very winning technique, all most a fine art, if you don't mind me saying so.'

'Not at all. Lady Brand. Indeed I am honoured by your kind remarks.'

There was a brief silence as Lady Brand toyed with her serviette.

'Have you kept him long?'

'Oh,' sighed Mistress Alexis, raising both hands to heaven in a gesture of approximation. 'About three years but I fear I shall have to retire him soon. He is getting inattentive and forgetful. Well, you have seen.'

'Where will he go when you let him go, as it were.'

'I have absolutely no idea. On the street I expect. Does it matter?'

'No, no, not at all. I hope this stain will come out of my shirt.'

Lady Brand's Kindness.

'In the context of a slave's life – kindness – (especially kindness shown by those privileged enough to hold the reins of the slave's existence) is not a form of relief but rather a superior expression and further layering of necessary cruelty. In the context of those destined by virtue of their genetic constitution on the one hand, or by virtue of their metaphysically determined karma on the other, to a life of "service", any apparent act of kindness on behalf of his ruler, his owner or Mistress or whatever nomenclature one chooses to employ is, as it were, and necessarily so, nothing more than a teasing and tightening of the reins, a refinement of the yoke of cruelty (as a given fact of his historical and manifest destiny), under which the servant must forever labour. In short, kindness (a discredited Christian virtue) is not to be seen as a form of relief but rather as a polished manifestation of a pragmatic and socially useful practice. Under these conditions, to those of us blessed with a sense of social responsibility, harshness and severity become not only a required modus operandi but also a civic duty. As such it represents higher form of pleasure known only to those adepts of humiliation, sensual intoxication/intimidation and social control whose happy evolutionary destiny it is to legislate and rule. All of which, it need hardly be said, is necessary for the establishment of the freedom, creativity and leisure of the Superior Gender. Indeed, in the long term even the gender deficient – the slaves themselves – will benefit from the freedom of those genetically disposed to make the best use of every higher liberty that only a proper ordering of society would allow.'

So wrote Lady Maria Estrela Brand in her last article for the *Woman's Home Journal*.

Standing in the kitchen prior to her departure, watching jonathan struggle with the dried up remains of Lady Brand's dinner, the author of those words was moved to demonstrate her own highly developed sense of civic duty.

As was the custom the slave was slurping his meal from a dog bowl placed on the floor. With great condescension Lady Brand crouched down beside him and gently tugged the bowl away.

'Let me have it, slave,' she said quietly. Standing up she placed the bowl on the kitchen table and using a dirty wooden spoon to stir the fish bones and dry vegetables Lady Kathleen Maria Brand M.A. PhD. spat five or six times into the mixture. She stirred vigorously.

'There' she said, placing the bowl under his nose once again. The added moisture will make it easier for you to eat.'

Alexis was towering over her servant.

'You may thank Lady Brand. Spittleflim.'

'Thank you, my Lady.'

Like summer lightning, Mistress Alexis stooped down and slapped jonathan very hard across his face.

'How dare you spittle? Lady Brand is **NOT** your Lady. Say thank you properly.'

His left cheek glowing red jonathan said.

'Thank you, Mistress Kathleen.'

'Good. Continue eating.'

Standing in the open doorway the two ladies embraced. Lowering her head Lady Brand tentatively offered Alexis her wet and parted lips softly glistening in the autumn moonlight.

Shyly Alexis accepted the fond farewell. Chuckling deeply, darkly in her throat Lady Brand deftly, quickly ran the tip of her tongue round the inside of Alexis's top lip. Alexis felt a shedder of delight pass through her body and then they parted.

'Thank you for a lovely evening, Alexis. Don't worry about your holiday in Paris. I am sure I can square it at the next board meeting.'

Looking askance down at jonathan still slurping his meal on the floor Lady Brand added.

'You simply must take a holiday, you have been working far too hard recently and deserve a break.'

Waving her hand and smiling, Lady Brand turned her back and disappeared down the short path- the form of her body dissolving like smoke with each step into the clean autumn air.

Closing the door Mistress Alexis said softly, 'Finish eating now; leave the rest of the dishes till tomorrow, wash your hands, face, clean your teeth and present yourself in the bedroom in five minutes.'

Madam Alexis stopped at the foot of the stair.

'Oh, and don't forget to turn out the lights.'

Five minutes later jonathan was in his owner's bedroom, kneeling, as was the ritual, at the foot of Madam's bed.

In every Superior household of every member of the Superior Gender the 'Auto Servitude Recliner' was a de rigueur piece of furniture.

Not only was it fashionable and serviceable in terms of needs – physical satisfaction and stimulation of the sympathetic nervous system – of the Mistress of the House but also, rigorous biological and social trials had shown, increased the passivity, obedience and all-round efficiency of the servant class subject to its daily employment.

The 'recliner' was in fact a simple double bed split three quarters of the way down into three separate units. These were two wide and comfortable leg supports to the left and\right of the bed with a narrow tail-piece of 'tongue' – as it was sometimes known forming the middle section.

Electronically controlled by a portable handset the outside 'arms' and inside 'tongue' could be raised and lowered at the whim of the Mistress by the simple pressing of a button.

The Mistress simply rested her spread legs on the arms – whilst the servant was required to lay chest down on the narrow tail-piece or tongue.

Chopin's Nocturnes were playing softly on the quadraphonic stereo system. Mistress Alexis lay under the black silk duvet. In time to the music Madam was murmuring a mantra/prayer to the Goddess of wealth and Power – Devanta. The room was in semi-darkness as the servant waited patiently for his owner to finish her prayer cycle.(Servants were not allowed prayers – conversation with the Gods being a privilege reserved only for the elect – beside which jonathan did not know the form of the mantra – all such knowledge nuggets being part of the secret freemasonry of the Ruling Matriarchy.)

Madam was wearing a blindfold of turquoise velvet and satin to ease her slide into sleep but from long practise she easily found the buttons on the remote. With hardly a sound save the muffled whirring of the machinery and the rustling of the silk sheets Madam's legs began to rise and the middle section of the bed lowered itself gently to the floor. The piano music faded and silence, virginal milk silence flooded stealthily into the room. Madam's spread and raised legs and sheets had created small tent aperture into which the servant now crawled. His head was nestling between her thighs. His mouth and nose a few centimetres away from the moist smell of her sex. Madam lowered her legs rests slightly and the servant felt the cool touch of freshly laundered sheets as they stretched across his shoulders.

From a long way off he heard the sleepy almost dull command.

'Get closer.'

He pushed his body further up the slope of the tail piece until his mouth was pressing hard against her labia = the end of his nose just touching her clitoris.

Madam gave a contented sigh as she heaved her hips and pubic bone into position. There was a silence for a few seconds. The servant began to panic as he thought she had already fallen asleep.

Then: 'You may begin.'

Nuzzling with his head nose, lips and tongue jonathan began to slowly lick, caress and lick her clitoris and suck, kiss and nibble her labial lips. After two or three minutes he forced his tongue between her crevice and began to lick and suck, lick and suck like a ravenous child at his mother's breast.

Mistress Alexis began to rotate her pelvic region, first to the right and then to the left. All the while she was thinking of Lady Brand and her 'special' farewell kiss.

Mistress Alexis squeezed her thighs around the servant's head. In turn he moved his head and kissed and licked her tender this, the sweet perfume of skin cream and must swirled into his cranium like a votive offering, like incense at a sacred rite.

Madam shuddered and\shuddered and shuddered again and again and again and then subsiding, she said quietly.

'Stop, servant stop'.'

His nose and mouth were drenched in her sticky essence.

He stopped. Hands by his side, head resting in her crouch, the wet smell of her sex still filling his head.

'You may withdraw, you may go to bed now.'

As best he could slave shuffled out backwards. As he did so a panel slid open in the wall opposite. Madam ad her fingers on the control button.

Behind the panel was a small concerted broom cupboard. A thin mattress of old cotton was rolled out in the narrow space between the sliding door and the wall. At one end there was a single off-white pillow. There was a thin grey duvet on the mattress. Jonathan crawled into the space and pulled the grey material up to his chin. Laying on his back he stared blankly into space. Beside the pillow there was one of Madam's disused high heel court shoes (a present) and on the pillow next to his head, folded neatly, there was an old seamed silk stocking (also a present).

Mistress Alexis pressed the button and the door slid to with a gentle click, and then the electronic lock snapped into place.

Outside he could just catch the whirring sound of machinery as his Mistress settled down for the night.

He was in utter darkness.

Blackness

And so ended the servant's day.

www.ingramcontent.com/pod-product-compliance
Lightning Source LLC
Chambersburg PA
CBHW041140170626
46815CB00007B/339